Finding Julia

Ha Phuong Chu Tran

with Judy Katz

Finding Julia

Published by HP Productions, Inc.

P.O. Box 3208

New York, NY 10163

714-290-4990

Library of Congress Cataloguing-in-Publication Data

Finding Julia

Ha Phuong Chu Tran with Judy Katz

Published by HP Productions

ISBN: 978-0-692-96712-6

Cover design by Westminster Press

Interior design by Tony Iatridis

Proofreading by Carol Nelson Falcone

Editorial assistance by Layla Baez

Table of Contents

Chapter One

A First Glimpse

The little out-of-the-way Vietnamese restaurant offered outdoor dining, and visiting American businessman Mike Chamonix had heard that the food was amazing. Tonight he sat at one of the al fresco tables, enjoying a cold drink and a delicious meal. He was taking some much-needed alone time tonight, to catch his breath from all the meetings and formal dinners. Now he could relax and really look around on this side street in the heart of Ho Chi Minh City.

Speaking of breath—there *was* an absolutely gorgeous young woman right at the other end of the row of tables that took his breath away. She was standing at the curb, talking to a little boy, one who could not be more than ten, if that. He was one of the hoards of children and old people who sold lottery tickets in the street to keep themselves alive. Although Mike did not understand Vietnamese, it was clear the undernourished child was telling the woman he was hungry. He watched as she brought the child over to a table, sat him down, and motioned the waiter to bring him a noodle dish. Interestingly, Mike had ordered that same dish, Hu tieu Nam Vang. It was filling and delicious.

As he watched, the small boy gobbled up the food and drank a big glass of water. Getting up, the child stretched out his hand to his generous and lovely benefactor, offering her his lottery tickets. She opened her purse and gave him some paper money, but refused to take the tickets. The boy walked away with a big grin on his pale face, and the generous soul sat down and resumed her own meal.

1

Could he approach this mysterious and lovely creature? Would he be intruding on her? Could she speak English? Mike gave up the internal struggle, paid his bill, and left. On the way, he approached the boy and gave him several small bills, but also refused the lottery tickets.

The next night, at the same hour, Mike was back at the same restaurant. Was she real, or a figment of his imagination? He had not been able to get the vision of her out of his mind and prayed that she was real ... and that she would be there once again.

There is a God! There she was, even more beautiful than he remembered. Again she sat at a distant table, quietly enjoying a light meal. As he watched her out of the corner of his eye, Mike saw her pause, put her chopsticks down, then get up and cross the street to approach a toothless elderly man, also selling lottery tickets. Holding out a thick wad of paper money, she handed it to the man but, as she had done the night before with the boy, refused the lottery tickets so he could sell them elsewhere. All the while she spoke to him in Vietnamese, in what was clearly a warm and encouraging tone.

Now Mike's curiosity was at an all-time-high. He had his camera with him, and although he would have loved to take her picture, he knew that would be intrusive. He would have to find out who she was some other way. Before he left the restaurant he subtly memorized everything he could about her: the piercing, intelligent dark doe eyes, the alabaster skin, the colorful dress that enveloped her slender and petite shape, and the long silky braid that flowed down her back.

He somehow knew he would never forget her. He had to find a way to meet this woman.

Mike belonged to a prominent Parisian family that had made its name in investment banking. Harvard had named a nursing school

2

after Mike's grandfather after his seven-figure donation—especially significant since it had been made at the height of the Depression. Returning to the United States after graduation from Harvard and INSEAD, where he received an M.B.A., he had done a brief stint at Morgan Stanley on Wall Street before venturing out on his own. He achieved immediate success. In just the first eleven weeks he had raised $250 million, a solid start for his eponymous hedge fund.

Mike's determination and ability to get results paid off. People who worked with him knew that he was restless—and relentless. He let nothing stand in his way when he was negotiating deals in London, Bonn, and Rome. From Wall Street to financial centers around the world, he built a reputation for working hard, dreaming big, and making things happen. His energy and ability doubled the value of his hedge fund in six months. *The Wall Street Journal* did a feature on him, and London's *Financial Times*, and *Forbes Magazine* put him on their cover.

Before his meeting, Mike Chamonix enjoyed his morning coffee and watched the sunrise from his penthouse suite in the Caravelle Saigon In.

Ho Chi Minh City. It was fascinating to look out at the skyline of rising Asia with its modern skyscrapers peppered with ornate temples and pagodas.

He also admired the wide elegant boulevards which were now starting to fill with the early morning scooter traffic. Soon they would be sweaty and bustling, the air filled with honks and shouts.

It was the city's energy and vitality that drew Michael Chamonix to it. With over seven million people, it flourished with prosperity rooted in tourism, finance, and foreign investment. The city was filled with a healthy young population whose eyes were fixed to the future. Green leafy *kapok* trees lined the streets. The chaotic rhythm of bicycles whisking ambitious young entrepreneurs through the streets fueled the city's adrenalin rush.

Checking his watch, Mike glanced at his appearance in the suite's foyer mirror as he waited for the private elevator. He had arrived here to wrap up a deal for financing a new construction venture, and he was never late.

Mike was a driven investor. He took pride in his ability to close any deal. Disciplined and focused, he was up every morning at 6:00 a.m., his designer shirts and suits impeccably pressed, his shoes shined perfectly. His Rolex wristwatch and gold cuff links lay in wait on the mahogany dresser. His world revolved around order, precision, detail, and he was *always* prepared for anything. He was a tough negotiator, strong but fair-minded, building bonds of trust among his associates. People knew that a deal he made with a handshake was as good as signing a written contract.

His natural ability to put others at ease made him a favorite with people from different cultures. Who wouldn't envy him, with his midnight-blue eyes, thick wavy hair and a ready smile?

 Peering out the limo window, Mike studied the rush of people his vehicle passed. A little girl in a floral-patterned traditional Vietnamese dress caught his eye as she waited for the street light to turn. Her smile was infectious as she held her mother's hand. Mike felt a pang of longing. The truth was, at the age of thirty, he was lonely. He loved children and looked on enviously when visiting the homes of friends as they tousled the hair of freckle-faced little boys and sweet girls in pigtails. In these little maps of innocence he saw hope and the promise of a good future. Mike prayed that one day he would have his own family.

But the right woman was elusive. The sea was filled with barracudas who saw Mike as a bottomless bank account. These women wanted him for his social standing and his money. Mike had no time for such women predators.

As he dreamed of having a family, he had even imagined the name that he would give to a child, one he hoped would be a daughter, for little girls had a way of bending him around their little fingers. In his mind, one name stood out for him: *Julia*. It honored his French heritage and its meaning was "youthful and feminine." He envisioned a daughter as delicate as a lotus flower and as beautiful as her mother. Having a loving wife and raising a child on whom he could lavish his love and affection was, he had to admit, what he fervently desired.

Arriving at his destination Mike snapped himself out of his daydream. He needed to conclude a deal to finance the construction of several new commercial and residential buildings in the city.

Mike was legendary in the finance world as a shrewd investor who paid attention to detail. Everyone in his industry knew that Mike had the ability to make things happen. Vietnam needed capital to move its shipping industry forward and Mike had the expertise and power to raise such capital.

Arriving at his destination, he was met by Dong Khanh, known in Vietnamese as Khanh Dong. In Vietnam, as with many Asian nations, the surname preceded the first name. He was also met by Quan Tram, Khanh's Chief Operating Officer, a slender man with a narrow face and intense dark eyes. For these negotiations, both colleagues and hosts wanted Mike to feel comfortable, so they adopted the American way of addressing one another. Mr. Khanh and Mr. Tram had insisted that Mike address them as Dong and Quan and Mike likewise asked them to address him by his first name.

At the end of the day the final details had been worked out and the contracts were approved. "I look forward to a long and prosperous relationship, Mike," Dong said, smiling, when the meeting concluded.

"Likewise, Dong," Mike replied with a radiant smile. "Vietnam is a proud nation, filled with great people and major accomplishments. I feel honored to count you both as new friends as well as colleagues."

Dong bowed his head, a gesture that Mike reciprocated. He looked at Mike.

"Yes, a golden future lies ahead of us." He turned his face to Quan and smiled. "We think you will enjoy our reception here this evening." Quan nodded in agreement. "We have a special guest: Phuong Ha," Quan added. "All of us and her many fans call her simply PH. She is a beautiful woman with an extraordinary voice."

"Phuong Ha is one of our nation's most celebrated vocalists," Dong added. "Our people adore her. She is one of those rare individuals who courageously speaks her mind and stands up for what she believes, even as she has established herself as a world-class artist. She never fails to move the hearts of anyone who hears her incredible voice." He uttered his extravagant praise in a reverential tone.

Mike could see that both Dong and Quan felt enormously proud of this performer and he anticipated an interesting evening.

"A nightingale could not have a more alluring voice," Dong expanded. "Hers is a divine gift from the heavens."

"She is elegant," Quan agreed with a twinkle in his eyes. "By the way, did I happen to mention she is not yet spoken for?" he slyly hinted with a meaningful nod to Mike.

Mike wasn't sure how to respond. It seemed as if they were trying to get some subtle message across. Their remarks aroused his interest. The past week of hard negotiations that had just ended left him a bit tired and in need of distraction. A festive evening of Vietnamese hospitality intrigued him.

The banquet took place in the ballroom at 8:00 that evening.

Cream silk curtains enveloped the windows, Aubusson carpets in rich hues enhanced the gorgeous marble floors, while waiters in white tuxedos served champagne and cocktails to the elite group of guests. The elaborately decorated room was crowded with men attired in formal black suits, while the women dripping in diamonds wore the latest fashionable gowns or formal traditional Vietnamese dress. Mike moved around the room, smiling and gracious, thanking his hosts. He made light small talk with various clusters of people before enjoying the delicious creations of some of Vietnam's most popular chefs.

Finally, the moment everyone had been anticipating. The lights dimmed and a spotlight arose upon Phuong Ha as she floated onto the middle of the stage. She was accompanied by a pianist who took his place at a Steinway piano, and two guitarists and a violinist who also seated themselves. After a musical introduction Phuong Ha began to sing. She had a deep, rich, robust voice. Her fluid body movements echoed the elegant melodies.

Like the rest of the audience, Mike was spellbound as she sang a folk ballad that Quan whispered to Mike was called "Farewell to the Past." While Mike could not follow the lyrics, he saw that they aroused tears. As he listened, Mike's pulse raced.

This was the beautiful woman he had watched in the restaurant. He could not believe it! Phuong Ha's voice and pleading dark eyes captured everyone's heart. Her silky dark hair trailed over her slender shoulders and down her petite, splendidly shaped figure. She was a heavenly vision in an elegant dark crimson red and black dress that graced her ankles. She was the same vision he had secretly watched the past two evenings in the little café.

As she sang, Phuong Ha's eyes connected with individual guests. As her eyes met Mike's, he felt an electric shock race through his body. Her eyes had fixed on Mike's face for nearly half a minute. She turned to other guests, then moments later shifted her gaze back upon him as the poetic song reached its climax. Every fiber in Mike's body pulsed with excitement. He was certain his eyes did not deceive him. *She was singing to him!* Her final gesture, palms stretched towards him, reinforced that conviction. Mike was breathless.

Mike had never bought into the possibility of love at first sight until now. This woman had captured his heart on the street when he had no idea who she was save for her gentleness and generosity. Now the feelings struck him like bolts of lightning. In a heartbeat this woman had turned him inside out. He felt light-headed and dizzy.

He turned to Quan. "You were right about this performer," he said, trying to keep his voice composed. "Who is she?" He wanted to know everything.

A shrewd judge of people, Quan could see that Mike was enchanted. He also had an instinct about how Phuong Ha would react to this fascinating American businessman.

Patiently he related PH's touching life story. "She came from humble origins," Quan explained, "and that has given her a sense of humility. Everyday people identify with her. She is one of them. They know she understands how they feel. She has dedicated her life and every success she achieves to them. Most of the money she earns goes to the poor. She gives hope to those who have none."

"I can think of few celebrities for whom that kind of humility and generosity would be true," Mike said.

Quan nodded. "PH is a most unusual woman."

"Exquisite," Mike mumbled, fixing his eyes on PH. The way she smoothly wove her arms in a fluid motion while swirling her hips in unison to the delicate melodies was beguiling. He admired her ability to create an entirely original artistic piece that blended voice, dance, and music. "You can feel the passion," Mike said, as she rendered a ballad called, "When Dreams Come". "She clearly loses herself in the melody," he continued.

Quan was equally moved. "There's no one like her," he said. Mike leaned in closer so as not to miss anything in the next ballad. The piano and strings accented her resonant voice. Clearly she felt deeply about the words she was singing.

"I can see why people love her," Mike observed as she finished her set. The crowd clapped and cheered.

"She is the most popular singer that Ho Chi Minh City has ever produced," Quan said.

"What's she like personally?" Mike inquired, trying to sound only mildly curious and not betray his avid interest.

"What exactly do you want to know?" Quan asked.

"She's dazzling as a performer, but what is she really *like?*" Mike wanted to know. Quan laughed but Mike was persistent. "Listen, Quan, in my world many of the stars I've come across boast big egos. They care for no one but themselves. Your Phuong Ha doesn't seem to be like that. I would just like to know more."

Quan laughed. "I have the pleasure of knowing her. She donates a portion of her performance fees to the foundation that she and her family created to help orphans."

"Can I meet her?" Mike asked pointedly.

"I'll gladly introduce you," Quan nodded.

"I'd like that," Mike beamed. His eyes were glued to the beautiful singer's every move as she warmly greeted other guests. Only a month before he had observed a famous movie star rudely deny a fan an autograph. PH was the opposite, cheerfully signing autographs for any guest who requested one.

When Quan finally introduced him to PH, Mike bowed his head in respect but couldn't resist smiling. To his delight, she returned his smile. Mike felt his body quiver as they made silent contact.

"Have you always sung?" he asked, his words tumbling out awkwardly—a first for a man never at a loss for the right words at the right time. "I see what you've achieved and I heard about your work with orphans. It's extraordinary."

Phuong Ha did not answer immediately. She had understood everything the handsome American had said, but her English was not fluent. She needed to make him understand why she hesitated in answering him.

"Forgive me. My English is not so good. I hope I can answer your question correctly." she said with a sweet smile.

"No need to apologize. I am in your country. I only wish I could speak your language," Mike replied. "And by the way, I love your accent."

"Thank you," PH said, pleased with the exchange. "And, yes, I have always been singing. Like a lot of young girls, I grew up dreaming to become a movie star. Unfortunately my father died of cancer when I was fifteen. My mother raised me and my two sisters. I know what it's like to be a child without a parent, even both parents. It's why I wanted for me and my family to start a foundation and help orphans. So many children in this country have already lost everything!"

"It is a wonderful thing you have done," Mike said with admiration. He meant it. It *was* a wonderful thing. "I'm sorry for your loss. Was your father also a singer?"

"No, but he was a successful musician and composer. It was he who had arranged for me to receive singing and dancing lessons in Ho Chi Minh City when I was much younger."

Her performance had confirmed that she was a natural. Smoothly integrated with the music, they had heightened the feelings she expressed—and despite her hesitancy about her English, she really had no trouble understanding the language or communicating back.

"I suspect that dancing with you would be like gliding across a ballroom floor in the arms of an angel," Mike said.

"You flatter me, Mr. Chamonix," PH blushed. She turned to Quan. "Americans are good at flattery, don't you agree?" Quan shook his head. "Ahh, but I think this one may be different."

PH looked Mike over from top to bottom. "He does have an honest face," she said playfully.

"And I'm wonderfully good-natured," Mike joked.

"So I suspect," PH flirted back.

Quan excused himself to speak with some other guests. It wasn't soon after, however, that PH apologized for having to leave as well. She was preparing for a national tour and long, arduous rehearsals were due to commence the following week. As with any accomplished professional, what looked spontaneous was the product of careful design and detailed, disciplined rehearsal. Mike took a breath and looked into her eyes. He felt as if he were meeting a woman whom he had known before. It was like she had always been there, waiting for him to find her.

"May I be forward?" he asked.

"How?" she asked, drawing back into herself.

"You say rehearsals won't start for several days."

"Correct."

He gulped, hoping he wasn't about to make a fool out of himself. *But what the hell*, he told himself. *Sometimes life gives you one chance.* He straightened up, fixing his tie, mustering up his courage, and implored her, "May I please have the honor of inviting you to lunch or dinner?"

His invitation neither rattled nor startled her. She looked at him for a moment, as if wondering whether to believe what her own heart was telling her. Then she smiled. "Yes," she said. "I would like that. I would like that very much."

They made plans to meet for lunch the very next day at Ciao Bella, among Ho Chi Minh's finest Italian restaurants. Mike liked Ho Chi Minh City but he also loved Northern Italian food. He could tell by her choice of restaurants that PH also had a cosmopolitan sensibility.

The next day, Mike sat nervously waiting for PH to arrive. Ciao Bello's red-tiled Tuscan floors, burnt orange interior, and dark wood chairs creating the cozy atmosphere of a Florentine café. Mike looked at his watch as he eagerly awaited PH's arrival. Suddenly she appeared in the doorway, the vision of loveliness. PH slowly crossed the room towards Mike. Seeing the look on his face, she lowered her eyes as her cheeks flushed pink. What he could not see was that she was trembling with anticipation.

They drank cold white Vernaccia di San Gimignano and shared a bowl of their signature dish, the "Posh Carbonara," and then baked sea bass. PH had a lithe figure, but, like Mike, she ate with gusto. PH knew the restaurant well and insisted they sample their famous tiramisu for dessert.

"Do you know the origin of the word *restaurant?*" he asked.

"Latin?" she speculated.

He shook his head. "French. *Restaurer* means 'food that restores.' It's about how good food restores the spirit."

"How do you know these things?" she wondered. Their hands brushed against one another.

12

"My mother was American, but my father was French." He shrugged wistfully. "My mind is filled with silly trivia like that. Anyway, I do believe our spirits have been restored," he said as they clinked glasses. "Especially in your company," he added. He couldn't speak for a moment, and when he did, found himself involuntarily stuttering. "This is special to me. Every minute I'm with you is special. I hope you don't mind my saying that."

She smiled, flattered. "I feel the same way," she said, her candor surprising herself. All of her training about showing restraint and caution in meeting new people had vanished. She made no effort to resist the impulse. Her words flowed out spontaneously.

As the meal progressed, they lowered the tone in their voices, and leaned in towards one another so as not to avoid missing a syllable of conversation. Besides her native Vietnamese, she spoke both English and French fluently. She explained that her prowess with languages stemmed from her education in a *lycee* to which her mother had arranged a scholarship.

"What about you?" she asked.

He grinned. "English, French, some Italian. Sometimes I wonder how well I speak English. My teachers claimed I had a knack for mispronouncing every other word."

"They were teasing you," she laughed.

"Easy for you to say. You were not the one they kept after school for detention and extra homework. Besides, I could hardly blame them. French was my first language."

"I thought you lived in New York," she questioned.

"Paris originally; we moved to the states when I was a teenager." He talked about his early years growing up in Paris. He had studied at the renowned Lycee Louis-le-Grand, which Voltaire had attended two centuries earlier. Later on, after they had moved to

New York, he continued to excel in his studies, eventually earning a scholarship to Harvard. Upon graduation, he attended a school for European elites based in Versailles.

"Versailles! That sounds very romantic," she said.

His face lit up as he recounted the experience. "INSEAD," as it was known, attracted the top students but when they weren't engaged in their studies, they partied night and day. Every year climaxed with an elegant formal at the Chateaux Vaux le Vicome, a baroque French chateau located in Maincy, just southeast of Paris. It was extraordinarily beautiful. Louis XIV's Finance Minister, Nicolas Fouquet, had engaged the famous architect Le Vau to design the stately chateaux and spacious grounds. He relayed to her the extravagant costumes they wore and the fun he had shared with his friends.

Her brow arched, "I see. And at these wild parties—did you behave yourself?"

"I behaved as you would expect any French student would behave," he said bemused.

"I doubt my mother would approve," she said, feigning disapproval.

"Mine didn't," he grinned.

She shifted topics to hide her vulnerability. "Do you consider yourself French or American?"

"French by background, but I consider myself a full-blooded American. What about yourself? Have you done much traveling?" he inquired.

"Here and there but I've never been to America. I hope to visit it one day," she replied.

"Well, I know of one American who would love to be your tour guide," he said tenderly.

They were speaking softly and it seemed that every moment that passed between them added a deeper gold to the aura that seemed to enshroud them. Phuong Ha has led Mike from one surprise to the next. As it turns out, her English is not as "not that great" as she humbly confessed when they first met. Up to this point in his life, Mike has met many talented and beautiful women, but none also has two qualities that Phuong Ha seems to possess naturally: the humility of a flower that simply emits her fragrance and a sincere desire to do charity work unassumingly. Those two qualities alone have made the woman sitting next to him right now a model of the Truth-Virtue-Beauty idea, a mysterious pulchritude uniquely Eastern, not just in character or outward appearance. He *loved* looking at her. Her slender hands, her beautiful skin, those haunting, penetrating eyes. She was everything he had ever imagined any man could want. He wondered what it might be like to have children with PH. Discretion being the better part of valor, he refrained from divulging that passing thought.

She was lost in her own thoughts. "I dream of doing movies in Hollywood, but I am Vietnamese. I'm never certain how well Americans accept foreigners. They say they do, but I am unsure. I think they like people who look like them and who sound like them."

Mike caressed her hands gently. "Americans are an open, generous people, but I confess there's an element of truth in what you say. America welcomes people of all cultures but sometimes, out of fear of those differences, prejudice rears its ugly head. He regarded her silently for a moment, then blurted out, "But I can tell you one thing, Miss Phuong Ha, any actor who would be lucky enough to hold you in his arms in an American movie, or in a Broadway show perhaps... would be one damned lucky man."

His words startled but didn't frighten her. "Oh yes?" she said. "Even to the point of forgetting who I am and where I came from?"

"No one could forget you. Not any part of you," he said. "I find that inconceivable."

"You are nice to say so."

"I mean every word." He reached out and took her hand, not thinking for a second that his gesture might be seen as being forward. The presence of PH cast a wonderful spell around him, and he was certain that as long as he could remain inside of it, nothing could hurt either one of them. His mind was so far from the rough-and-tumble world of business that he might have been in a different universe. He felt a jolt of new excitement when she allowed him to clasp her hand, keeping her gaze fixed firmly upon him.

Deliberately calming himself, Mike let her hand go and took a sip of his wine. One thing he felt strongly about—he knew he had to dispel her doubts about Americans. It was that or probably she'd never see him again. What would be the point? He drew a breath.

"It's the effort and the heart that counts. When people come to the U.S. and accept American values—support your neighbor, work hard for success, respect the individual—and want to be *American*, they are welcomed." He paused. "I don't know about you as an actress, but I can say without a moment's doubt that as a singer you'd be a mega-star in the States. Your work with children would amplify your standing. People would reach out to you with their hearts and their souls. The people who make it are those for whom their art is self-expression. Yours certainly is. It's infectious, PH, and goes beyond differences in culture or language."

"Thank you," she said. She looked at him in astonishment, both amazed and delighted. "I believe you mean that." She had to admit he wasn't like any man she had ever met. He showed respect and treated her as an equal.

She also found him attractive, in a curiously exotic way. His

16

midnight blue eyes were pools of mystery that intrigued her. She also had to admit that she longed to glide her fingers through his thick wavy hair, clasped in his embrace and inhaling his woodsy musk cologne. She loved the touch of his hand.

His eyes seemed to dance as he looked at her. She trembled, her blood flowing with tides of warm sensation.

After lunch, she suggested they walk together in Tao Dan Park, where a reflecting pool filled with lily pads boasted sweet white flowers, bench-lined walks full of tall tropical flame trees and Sao Den trees that provided tranquility and beauty. They stopped at a small kiosk and had strong, rich, dark espresso. She noticed that he stirred a lot of sugar into his cup. "Are you having espresso with sugar or is it the other way around?" she teased.

"I have a sweet tooth," he confessed. "I love croissants, cakes, and cookies. It's bad for my waistline but I can't help myself. You?"

She laughed. "I'm a performer. I have to watch what I eat." She signaled to the kiosk owner and ordered a slice of chocolate cake with two forks. As the owner brought them over, Mike saw that they were generous slices of richly textured cake with thick icing.

"About your being a performer..." he started to tease.

She raised a hand. "For you, Mike, I make an exception."

Just then two young children, a boy and a girl, ran across in front of them, chased by a frantic parent. Mike and PH laughed. "I know you love children," he said, "Do you want your own some-day?"

"Yes, absolutely," she said. "I definitely plan to have my own little ones, when the time is right."

"How many?" he wondered. The words were out of his mouth before he could catch himself. He felt he should have pinched his arm. *How could he be asking this famous person a question like this on their first date?*

"Two," she said without hesitating. "You?"

"Three. I especially want a daughter."

She leaned forward and whispered with a curious smile, "Let me guess. You already have a name picked out."

Mike blushed. The smartest business people on the planet liked to comment that his poker face made him impossible to read. One lunch with Phuong Ha and she seemed to have memorized the blueprint of his brain. She could read him like a book. He sliced a morsel of cake and held it up to her lips. She took the fork from him, ate the small piece of cake and nodded approval. "Delicious," she said. She picked up a forkful of cake and held it to his lips. "You next." When he opened his mouth and reached for the mouthful, she flirtatiously pulled it away, "First though, the name."

His eyes widened and he gave a shy smile. "Julia."

Her face lit up. "That is a beautiful name," she said quietly, feeding him the cake ever so delicately.

"You like it?" he replied chewing a mouthful of the sweet confection.

"Very much. It is both elegant and feminine, with a hint of determination."

"It's meaning is 'youthful and mesmerizing' but in the Latin version it means 'soft hair'," Mike said. They both laughed. "Either way, I've always loved the name," he continued.

Later, as they walked through the park, he grasped her soft hand in his, hoping she didn't notice his sweaty palms. She only let out a contented sigh and smiled. Soon they came upon a group of old men carrying beautiful bamboo cages. PH bowed to the men and spoke to them gently in her language. They nodded and she promptly pulled something from her pocket and began dropping cracker crumbs into the cages. "What are you doing?" Mike asked.

"Feeding the birds," she laughed. "You do not have birds in your America?"

"I don't know if you could call the pigeons in Manhattan 'birds'; they're more like pooping machines," he offered. She laughed at his silly joke and he loved to hear the sound of it: a laugh that is so melodic it's like a song in itself. He made a mental note to start learning some jokes just to hear her laugh again.

They walked along the pathways, breathing in the perfumed scent of the gorgeous floral gardens with their alluring koi ponds.

"Your country has a lovely culture," he noted. "The people are polite, kind, and full of hope."

"Vietnam looks to the future," she said.

"Tell me about your work with orphans."

"I want every child to have the same opportunities I did. I'm committed to making that happen."

He stopped to purchase a lotus from a vendor and handed it to her. "In our country, giving a flower is a sign of friendship."

She accepted it and smiled. "Mike Chamonix, you surprise me. Why is it I feel that in the space of a single day our souls may have met in another lifetime?"

"Perhaps they did," he said. "I suspect it is a fact."

She smelled the fragrance of the lotus. "For us, the lotus is a symbol of divine beauty. It stands for purity, serenity, and optimism."

"Like the beautiful woman holding it in my presence."

"Like the handsome man whose gallantry prompted a beautiful gesture."

They smiled at one another and without thinking, joined hands even more tightly as they walked around some breathtaking sculptures. Mike had always wondered what his most perfect day would be like, if he ever had one. Now he had his answer. It was to spend time in a park full of the fragrances of flowers, songbirds, luscious green shrubs along the rippling waterfalls of the water gardens, decadent chocolate cake—and Phuong Ha. Above all—Phuong Ha. He felt like the luckiest man on earth. Indeed, he knew that, at least for the moment, he was. He looked into her dreamy eyes and saw paradise.

Chapter Two

Two months elapsed before Mike and PH reunited. Mike struggled with his emotions while he was away from her. Every hour of every day without her felt like an eternity. Nothing could fill that void. They exchanged emails or text messages almost every day, but that was not satisfying. Even while she was on tour around Vietnam with her concerts, she found time to contact him. They closed many days and nights with a twenty minute conversation on their phones, finding ways to make it work despite the time differences.

When they came back together, it was in Vietnam, and they celebrated at Ciao Bella, in homage to the place that had brought good karma. The expression of their love required no words. They felt as if they occupied the same dimension in space and time as soulmates. He loved every part of her. He loved looking at her. He loved the lyrical sound of her voice. He loved the way she looked at him. Above all, he felt both humility and gratitude that she was in love with him.

For her part, his warm heart and unstinting love evoked a passionate response. Every time she was with him the world felt right. He was now ready for the next step—the proposal. But of course this would not be simple. First, he would need to ask her mother's approval. And Van Tran, for whom Mike had the greatest respect, would not make this easy. She was the protective mother of a very special daughter who was also a celebrity with a career taking off by leaps and bounds.

Van had dined with Mike several times. She found him quite charming and could see why her daughter loved this man. Still, she felt there were major hurdles. Together she and Mike had spent time openly discussing PH's future.

"If you marry, then my daughter would have to live most of the time in America," Van declared. "That worries me. She does speak English well enough, but she has a history and a career here. Starting over will not be easy for her."

Mike nodded. "I can understand why any mother would be alarmed at the prospect of a daughter living in another country—especially one as remarkable and successful as Phuong Ha. It was a challenge that my own mother faced when she married my dad and moved from New York to Paris," Mike admitted.

"But it worked out?" Van asked.

"It did," Mike said.

"People from different cultures face special challenges."

"Love is what makes surmounting them possible," Mike said. "As I said, my parents did."

Van appraised Mike carefully. She had watched Mike and Phuong Ha as they sat in the garden of her modern concrete and glass villa in Thach My Loi, part of Ho Chi Minh City. They clearly couldn't take their eyes off one another. At the same time, they clearly respected the strict protocols of propriety, a point that resonated well with Van. She could see them from her study—they were slightly hidden behind the trees in the lush green garden, just holding hands. The spacious home and gardens were ideally suited for private gestures, beyond hand holding, but even seemingly unobserved they were respectful of her and of each other.

Van reveled in the fact that Mike made PH happy. Her lovely and talented daughter was generally a happy person, but with this American entering her life, she had become not just a girl but a woman. It was obvious that however polite they might be to the rest of the world, the one thing they wanted to have time for was each other.

The two spent time in silence for a few minutes, taking in the refreshing breeze and the sound of a black songbird with red cheeks, chirping a melodic tune, keeping time with the tinkling of the wind chimes.

Finally, Van fixed Mike with a firm look. "I can sense that you have a true heart and that you love Phuong Ha," she said in a serious tone.

"With all my heart. With all my soul."

"I understand. I believe you. But as you know, Phuong Ha is strong-minded and follows her own heart. She is the person you need to convince. If she wants the marriage, and to move to your country with you, then you have my blessing, Mike."

Keeping her own counsel, Van decided that she would have a private conversation with her daughter, to see what was truly on her mind. Was she really ready to make such an enormous change, and perhaps abandon the career she had worked so hard to achieve, for the love of this one man?

****

Early the next morning, at breakfast, mother and daughter sat across from one another silently over tea. Mike was staying in their guest house, but had journeyed into the city for a meeting. The two women studied each other, seeming to know each other's thoughts. PH could be impulsive with her career because spontaneity was crucial to her artistry. In her personal life, however, she took time to ponder her future. In discussing the prospect of building a life with Mike, having children with him, and surmounting the cultural divides between East and West, she was solemn and thoughtful.

Like Mike, she had known from the moment she laid eyes on him that he was the one. She knew they would share eternal love, if such a thing was possible. It was about much more than wanting Mike in her life: she could not imagine life without him.

Her mother minced no words about her concerns. "I like Mike," she said. "He is everything you said. I cannot argue. His character is not what concerns me."

"What does, mother?"

"The unfamiliar new life you will have to live in another part of the world, far from family and friends. The loss of momentum for your career. The different language and customs. Things like that worry me for you, my beloved daughter."

PH had already considered those issues. "You raise valid concerns, mother, but I have thought them through, and they are surmountable. I know in my heart that with my tenacity and Mike's support it will all work out. I know Mike. He values me as his equal and cherishes me for who I am and not for how many albums I sell or magazine covers I am on. I want to build a life with him. I want to bear his children. We will stand together as a family. Please know that I will always want to make you proud, mother, and I shall."

Seeing that Van had tears in her eyes, PH stood up, walked around to Van's chair, and bent over to hug her. "Trust me to make the right decision in matters of the heart. This is not the end of something, but an exciting new beginning."

Van regarded her, then slowly nodded her head. "Okay, daughter. You have my permission to follow your heart and marry this man. It has clearly already been decided by the gods on high. I only hope the sacrifices you make will not be too much for you to bear. You are my precious child. If you do move to America I will visit you as often as fate allows—if you want me to."

"You honor me, mother. It goes without saying that any home of mine will always be a home of yours if and when you want it."

Van bowed her head and the two embraced.

The wedding took place a few months later. It was a huge affair, the ceremony held outdoors amidst the lush gardens alive with the heady scent of lotus flowers and the swish of fat fish in the koi ponds. The stellar reception was held in several wide tents spread out over an acre on the back of an estate owned by close friends of PH's mother and late father. Members of this wealthy family had watched Phuong Ha blossom into a wonderful young woman and were proud to offer their grounds for the auspicious event. PH looked absolutely stunning in the ivory Vera Wang gown that Mike had ordered custom-made for her in New York. It was a form-fitting mermaid gown with a sweetheart bodice embellished with freshwater pearls. Her luscious jet black hair had been swept up and adorned with little white flowers and pearls with a long veil trailing behind.

The marriage of one of their country's biggest celebrities was news, and the ceremony and reception were covered on Vietnamese television. Despite the 800 people in attendance and the television crews, the affair had a warm intimate feeling. The fact that the groom was a Westerner might have been expected to upset some people, but no negativity was in evidence: the love the bride and groom had for each other was abundantly clear, and everyone fell under their spell. At one point Mike got up and made a short speech for his bride, using a few Vietnamese expressions, but with such a bad accent that everyone laughed. Phuong Ha, for her part, walked up to a microphone and sang a beautiful love song for her new husband, thrilling Mike, the large assemblage of guests, and later, the vast Vietnamese television audience.

After returning from their blissful two week honeymoon in Paris and Rome, the plan was for Phuong Ha to move to New York with Mike and make that her permanent home—with of course frequent visits back to perform and to spend time with Van. They applied for PH's visa, and were making preparations when fate intervened: Van, who had always had a mild heart condition, grew increasingly short of breath, and, as it turned out, would require heart surgery and a long recuperation period. Phuong Ha stayed to help care for her, while Mike returned to the U.S, for business, going back and forth regularly. On one return visit, he received exciting news: he was going to be a father!

Their infant daughter, Julia, was everything they could have hoped for: a lovely little girl with dark eyes and silky hair who closely resembled her mother but with her father's skin tone and the shape of his face. She was an exceptionally good baby, sleeping through the night almost from the beginning. Van was crazy about her, and spent a good deal of time talking to her in Vietnamese. In fact, both Van and PH spoke mostly Vietnamese to the child, and the nanny they brought in to help was Vietnamese. When they did speak English to the little girl, it was with a heavy accent.

Mike hoped that once the family moved to the United States his daughter would become fluent in English. However, Van took a long time to return to health, and Phuong Ha was in no rush to emigrate: she remained busy with her frequent concerts, television performances, and the albums and videos she recorded. She travelled to New York with Mike several times over the next few years, but it was not until Julia's fourth birthday that the little family was able to make their permanent transition. One aspect they had planned for years, and that an immigration attorney facilitated, was Van coming to live with them. Her health had improved, and she was far too attached to her daughter and little Julia to stay behind. She also now loved Mike with all her heart as well.

Chapter Three

Bundled in her fox fur coat and hat, Phuong Ha rested comfortably in the Lincoln Continental's back seat, reflecting on the state of her career, as she had been doing with increasing frequency lately. She had only been in the United States permanently for one year, and her albums and videos were still popular in her native land, where her hauntingly melodic voice had brought her so much adoration and success in her thirty-two years on earth. However, given Mike's hectic travel schedule, and his desire to have her join him for his frequent forays around the world on their private jet, this past year she had not had time to return home to perform.

Although she loved her new life, and loved her husband madly, as time passed she feared that she would be forgotten in Vietnam. No amount of reassurance by her mother, Mike, and her Vietnamese talent manager tried to allay her concerns. She worried that giving only one concert a year—or perhaps not even one a year—in her native country was not enough to maintain her popularity.

Besides telling her she would not be forgotten and that they would find a way to get her back to Vietnam more often, Mike also urged her to keep up with her new voice and drama coaches in Manhattan and work at building a singing and acting career in America.

In only a short time in New York City, she had made some progress. At first, she was known only as Mrs. Michael Chamonix. But as she began to make appearances for charities, people found her music different and refreshing. Many pleaded with her to record in the U.S. Her folk-based Vietnamese music was fresh and innovative. She had also learned some American "covers" —popular English-language songs sung by others that she was able to make her own. She conveyed deep emotion, passion, and integrity.

Her emotions were especially powerful as she sang or talked about families, especially children as the face of the future. Recently she had given a private concert for them that had raised significant funds for the United Nations International Children's Emergency Fund (UNICEF). Her intent was to raise awareness not only for UNICEF but also for the charitable foundation she had established in Vietnam to help orphans by giving them shelter, nutritional food, and comfortable clothing as well as educational opportunities. On these occasions people recognized that her commitment was sincere. She drew them in. She spoke eloquently about the challenges that confronted orphans. She extolled the sacred obligation to help needy children be safe, secure, and to realize their full potential. Rarely did she speak without shedding a tear. Her strength and power conveyed a majesty that moved audiences and motivated them to become involved.

PH never regretted marrying Mike. Yet her transition from the role of superstar to wife and mother, was bittersweet. Perhaps someday Julia would be as ambitious as she, and inherit her twin desires: to entertain the world with Vietnamese songs as well as English ones, and to help orphans and other lost children, so that they too had every opportunity to develop their minds and their talents, and grow up to lead happy and productive lives.

Julia was now five, and had only been among English-speaking people for the past year. While PH planned to take Julia back to Vietnam often as she grew older to make sure she appreciated her heritage, and generally spoke her native tongue to her child, she realized that Julia would need to become fluent in English. This year she was entering Kindergarten at an exclusive private school, and both parents were assured the teachers would help her with any language challenges. The important thing was that Julia was a happy child and knew how much she was loved and adored.

****

PH sat in the back seat of their luxurious car, swathed in a fur blanket, watching out the back side window at how much snow had fallen just since they started home. With Mike at the wheel, the family was on their way back into the city from a weekend at their sprawling country home. Warm and snug, PH rested her head against the smooth leather of the spacious sedan. She clasped her arm around Julia. Safely secured with a seat belt, Julia rested comfortably against her mother, her small face buried in the fur. Lost in a daydream, half-asleep after a full day in the country, the motion of the car lulled her into sleep.

Moving slowly along the snow-covered side streets, the car stopped at a light. Phuong Ha opened her eyes and caught her husband's glance. Their eyes met in the rearview mirror and she smiled at him.

"Glad you're getting some rest, honey," Mike said quietly, so as not to disturb Julia. "We still have long way to go. The snow is slowing us down. But no worries—we'll get there before dark, and Van will make sure the staff has a warm fire waiting for us, and something delicious for dinner."

Mike had many private names for her, but Mike preferred addressing his wife as PH. PH had taken hold with the couple's extended circle of friends and social acquaintances. Phuong Ha was a woman of strength and determination. She had a vision for herself, her husband, and her daughter. She resolved to fulfill that vision. No obstacle, no matter how difficult, could—or would—stop her from realizing it. That vision that was rooted in love, happiness, and an optimistic view of what was possible for the future—since she was always one who kept her eyes focused firmly on the future. Right now she was more determined than ever to prevail through her challenges.

PH again gazed out the tinted windows at the falling snow. It had begun lightly but now it was really coming down, and the temperature had dropped. In the driver's seat, Mike could feel that the roads were becoming treacherously icy. He looked concerned as he steered the car slowly around some sharp curves along the narrow suburb streets they were still on.

Although he rarely did so for their frequent weekends, Mike had given Tony, their driver, this Sunday off, telling PH that he preferred to drive them home himself. He was just in the mood to get behind the wheel for a change and enjoy the smooth ride along the country roads, he told his wife before they left. Only a light sprinkling of snow had been predicted, and he felt he could easily handle that. After giving her a passionate kiss on the lips with an enticing, hungry look that spoke of a great night ahead, he had opened the back car door so she could snuggle in with Julia.

PH had no concerns about Mike driving them home, although she didn't love the unexpected severity of the weather he now had to contend with. Mike had excellent reflexes and a natural feel for navigating difficult conditions. He had achieved success through focus, discipline and the ability to think about things in a way that always took the other person's viewpoint into account. He was strong. He made PH feel safe. PH felt confident in the knowledge that, with her husband at the wheel, even in this bad weather, their safety was assured.

Julia sat up and looked at her mother with a bright smile. PH leaned down and kissed her on the forehead. The precocious five-year-old's face glowed, and she snuggled closer to her beloved mother. Hugging her even tighter, PH gazed at the back of her handsome husband's head as he drove them through the winter storm.

Mike watched the streets with alert eyes. Fortunately there was almost no other traffic on these narrow side streets. Through the overhead mirror his eyes met PH's again, and Mike blew his wife a kiss. Turning his head for an instant, he smiled at the sight of his little girl, her face deep in the fur, and his heart swelled.

As the car steadily drove through the neighborhoods, they passed many brightly lit houses—it was almost Christmas, and in the windows of many homes on could see Christmas trees, sparkling with ornamental lights. Meantime the steady swish of the windshield wipers drummed on in the silence. Mike reflected back on the last five years and thought how lucky he was to have found PH. He realized that in the eyes of those who did not know them, or whose vision was too narrow, they seemed an unlikely match. But there were also subtle similarities—they were both ambitious and hard-working—although he felt guilty when his wife openly feared that she might soon be forgotten in Vietnam, or expressed doubts about her ability to make it as a performer in America.

PH was a star in the performing arts, while Mike had achieved his own fame in business and finance. They were both stars, bound in mutual respect for the extraordinary ability that each other possessed, and by their boundless love for one another, and now for their daughter Julia. Julia, of course, was the light of their lives. Her arrival cemented their bond. They were committed to giving everything they had to Julia. Mike constantly referred to his daughter as the "apple of his eye," an American saying that resonated with PH and their friends. He also frequently addressed her as "Princess." PH was his queen, and Julia was, truly, his little princess.

As the car made its way towards the expressway that would take them back to the city, PH shuddered involuntarily and audibly sighed. From the front seat Mike tried to reassure her, "Relax, darling," he said. "We'll be home soon."

"We should have waited out the storm," PH nervously cautioned him.

"Couldn't," he said. "I have to get back tonight. Rostex Technology's deal is on deck to close. The lawyers insisted on meeting at eight tomorrow morning. I need to review the documents this evening, and be there very early." He let out a frustrated sigh of his own. He preferred walking into a room, asking his counsel if everything was in order, getting the green light, and then just signing. But he knew that understanding the details of every element of complicated deals would make or break them, especially in this case. He wanted to avoid any last minute glitches with such a demanding client.

"Is it lawyers who make this trouble for you?" his wife asked. "Maybe you need to show them who is boss!" she joked.

"It's not the lawyers," Mike grinned at his wife in the rearview mirror. PH was kidding, but he knew there was a disciplined woman with an iron will inside that soft exterior.

"No?" she asked with one raised brow.

He shook his head. "It's Jack Rollins, the CEO and honcho at Rostex. Roilins says we close tomorrow afternoon or the whole thing's off. It's a $500 million deal. Putting this together has taken months. I'm not letting this one slip through my fingers."

"We don't need the money," PH shot back.

"Maybe not," he agreed. "Honey, I'm thinking of the foundation you and Van started. Your generosity rescues children who would grow up with such terrible disadvantages. Without you those orphans would be forgotten and lost. It offers them the promise of much better lives. I want to do everything I can to bring in more contributions, to make your foundation stronger, and to help more children. It's the least I can do to help." He uttered those words with great sincerity. Sharing her concerns about children was one of the many reasons that she had fallen in love with this handsome and brilliant man, and found, day by day, that her love and respect for him only deepened.

"Okay, I understand, darling, just be careful," PH replied. She pressed her face closer to the window, watching the snow come down and humming a folk tune near her child's ear, to give her sweet dreams. The icy road conditions made her clutch her child closer while singing her a lullaby that she often sung on stage.

Mike was aware of the drastic changes PH had faced after their marriage. His work took him to many countries and the constant traveling took a toll on PH. Although she did it willingly, she understandably also felt a loss of her original home, its people, and its traditions. She loved the optimism that had become its trademark. Vietnam had emerged from the ashes of war in 1975. It went through a difficult period of transition. But especially since 2000, it had grown and evolved and become a jewel among cities in Asia. Indeed, the optimism and high spirits of its people served as a source of inspiration for PH's own art.

Now Phuong Ha had a new life and a new reality. Michael had promised to treat her like royalty. He made good on that promise every day, and treated her like a Queen. He spared her no luxury, yet the loss of her regular schedule of performances and recordings in Vietnam weighed on her, and made her sad. Fortunately such blue periods were infrequent and Julia always seemed to bring her spirits up. Nonetheless, she secretly harbored ambitious plans for a professional comeback, thinking of ways in which she could better balance both family and an international career.

An image flashed through her mind. It was the excitement among fans at a stadium concert she had given a few years back in Ho Chi Minh City. Young people had filled the stadium. Her singing had made them delirious.

"Phuong Ha! Phuong Ha! Phuong Ha!" the crowd cried as she took her fifth curtain call. The lilt in her voice always evoked raw emotions. The audience had moved to her sweet melodies and contemporary beat. The first note that left her lips had stirred each of her fans. They swayed and cheered after every number. Cameras snapped pictures and brief videos. Those who attended the event would remember and talk about it for a lifetime. PH enjoyed the revelry. Its absence had left a gap in her life that she promised herself she would find a way to bridge, and still be a great and loving wife and mother.

The snow had reduced their speed to a snail's pace. Mike glanced at his wife again through the rear view mirror, observing her carefully. "I've seen that look on your face before," he said. "You look troubled. What's bothering you, darling?"

PH clasped Julia tightly. "Nothing. Nothing at all, really Mike."

"It's your music—your career—isn't it?" He glanced over his should to show he was paying attention. He quickly turned back to the road ahead, but kept talking. "Why wallow about in regrets? You have so much to be thankful for. Your life—*our* life—lies ahead of us. You can return to the stage and the studio here in New York. I can help make that happen, and I would love to!"

"No," PH declared. She forced a smile. "I love you for your support, Michael" —for her, he was always *Michael*. "But soon they will forget about me in Vietnam. My fans, they will feel they will never see me again. And here, in America, they do not know me. They see me only as your wife. I am—how do you say it—an ornament."

"Nonsense, PH," Mike insisted. "I've said it before and I'll say it again. You are still a star there, and you can be one here too. Record another album. Include your own compositions. You have the voice of an angel and the spirit of a great poet. Americans will find you unique. They'll love you."

PH took pride in her art. But this country had its own traditions and culture and its own preferences. She appreciated Mike's support. Yet for all of his encouragement, she understood the challenges in moving from her native culture to America's.

"You mean well, Michael. But Americans do not know Vietnamese music, and will not find it generally appealing, except perhaps to a few." she replied in a firm tone. PH had a romantic streak, but in business she prided herself on being a realist.

"How do you know until you try?" he asked. "You got to where you are never giving up or giving in. Follow your heart. Listen to it. Your art flows from what is buried deeply within your soul."

He smiled, then reached back to touch her. He was determined that she would have every opportunity to achieve her dreams. He knew that her success was important for Julia. Their success—his and PH's—would lay a solid foundation for the future that Julia could build upon.

Mike was resolute. "I will build a professional recording studio out in Westchester. We'll put in the best equipment. We'll hire the best engineers and backup singers. You will do an album. It will be your best work ever."

She smiled back at him: her number one supporter! "Do you really think so, Michael?"

He nodded. "Without a doubt. We will hire the top people to

market it. You will receive the fame in America that you deserve."

Mike gestured expansively with one hand on the wheel. "The music world has gone global. Look at *Vietnam Idol*. It's part of the *Idol* franchise. You know what gigantic hits the Idol shows are here and in Great Britain. Vietnam television has made it a hit in your country. Put your own mark on Vietnamese music. Be bold."

He looked at her through the mirror. "You're a star. The secret is to let people see you. They went wild from Ho Chi Minh City to Hanoi the instant you appeared. They'll do the same from New York to San Francisco. Have faith."

A tiny tear had formed around her eye. The topic was emotional. "But what you predict will most likely not happen. I'm Vietnamese. Americans like what they know."

"Americans like what they discover," Mike countered. "America opens its heart to those who open theirs to them. Your talent is a priceless gift—one that everyone will admire."

PH shrugged wistfully. "Maybe," she agreed doubtfully. Looking out the window at the snow that was enshrouding the roadways and covering the grass and trees with a thick blanket of whiteness, she consoled herself with a happy thought that fortune had smiled upon her. It had blessed her with an impregnable marriage, fortified by their beautiful young daughter. Soon they would arrive safely home. There her beloved mother Van, along with the Vietnamese couple who took care of the spacious apartment, would have a warm meal waiting—perhaps their delicious signature Vietnamese *Pho*, a rice noodle-based soup filled with beef or chicken and herbs.

The prospect of arriving home cheered her spirits. PH's mood was infectious. Julia awakened and picked up on it instinctively while happily snuggled up against her mother.

PH stroked Julia's head and focused on her schedule. She would devote a good part of it to making sure her daughter got help with her English.

Julia shared many of her mother's qualities. When they took Julia with them on their travels she soaked up every experience. She appreciated the exotic and unique. She took joy in the unforgettable moments she shared with her parents. But Julia needed to feel at home in the U.S. Although half Caucasian, her mother's genes rendered her a true child of Asia. Julia would have to come to terms with America, who she was, what she was, and how she fit it. That was important in gaining acceptance among Americans.

PH had recently hired Sarah, a special English tutor, a charming graduate student, for herself, to help her improve her own vocabulary and enunciation. Although the individual attention had helped Phuong Ha she still struggled. English is a difficult language to master unless it's your first language. Even the most gifted found mastering any foreign language a challenge once they reached beyond early childhood.

"What is my problem?" PH had wondered.

"A familiar problem," Sarah said. "Especially for Asians who come to America. The enunciation is different. Take the way the two cultures handle names. Americans put the first name first. Vietnamese—most Asians—do the opposite. Their surnames come first."

"Yes, but it's more than that," PH had said.

"Of course," Sarah had nodded. "English has a lot of slang. People make up new words every day. Old words acquire new meaning. Learning English as a formal language is tough enough, but the nuances of English are complicated."

"Yes, that makes sense."

"Fear of failing is the demon," Sarah said. "Have faith. You will do fine. You are someone *who will not quit.*"

Remembering this conversation, Phuong Ha laughed aloud,

rousing Julia out of her light sleep. As she awoke and looked deeply into her mother's eyes Julia's smile spread across her face. Phuong Ha's eyes, looking back at her with such love, would be forever etched in her memory. In that instant the car's front wheels hit a patch of black ice and skidded across the center dividing line of the narrow country road. As if in slow motion the car spun around—just as headlights of a Mac truck shown upon them. The driver honked loudly, but it was too late for either to stop: the vehicles collided, mangling the car bodies and shattering glass. Their lighter vehicle was thrown forward and smashed into a tree.

"JULIA!" PH cried out. It was a primal scream, as she desperately tried to shield her daughter from the eminent impact. Mike lunged for his wife. Then all became eerily silent. Coming to his senses, Mike unbuckled his seat belt with shaking hands, crawled out from behind the air bags on the front and side of him, ripped open the twisted rear door and found Phuong Ha holding Julia in a protective hug. PH's eyes were open, her head dangling at an odd angle. Instinctively, he knew her neck was broken, and that she was gone. Mike reached for Julia, cocooned in her mother's arms. He had to tear her away. Experts later estimated that, on the 25 mph country road, the truck had been zooming at 40 mph. Its driver had been half-dozing at the wheel. Too late, he realized that a car was skidding into its path.

"Mama, mama, mama thức dậy," Julia cried, lapsing into the Vietnamese term for "Wake up." "Daddy, please, make mommy wake up," she pleaded with him between sobs. She grabbed her mother's arm and pulled on it, but PH's lifeless body did not move.

Holding her tightly, a dazed Mike pulled his crying daughter from the wreckage and carried her through three feet of snow in case the car might explode in a fiery blaze. Thankfully it did not. From the side of the road he heard the dazed trucker call out that the police and an ambulance were on the way. Soon the sound of sirens cut through the air. A flood of tears washed over Mike's face. Holding Julia against his shivering chest, he hugged her tightly, hanging on for dear life. In a moment, their lives had unraveled.

Chapter Four

Sixteen Years Later

Acting class was in full session, and Julia was on stage. "Let me guess!" Julia, playing the role of Anh, the Vietnamese wife of U.S. Senator Don Hawkins, said. "He told you he was a bachelor?" Julia had been working hard to understand the role she was playing, understand the character, and above all, to get her lines down pat. Her language tutoring was paying off. She gritted her teeth and eyed the other actress as if it confronting the Devil. "And you believed him? You thought he was telling the truth? Why would you believe that? He's married—married to *me!*" she shrieked.

"He claimed he was getting a divorce," The actress playing opposite her yelled back. It was the role of Tiffany, played by a classmate named Vicky, a slim, attractive blonde wearing a fashionable red dress, three-inch designer heels, and diamond stud earrings. Vicky's attire was Upper-East-Side-chic. "He swore it to me!" She looked up, breaking character. "Wait, who is this again?" she asked, confused. Vicky's over-acting made her look silly.

Vicky scowled and threw Julia a sideways glance. Everybody could see that Julia had natural acting ability. Her body language conveyed strength. Her firm jaw and mouth—consciously twisted to emphasize visible anger—added strong theatrical notes. The only weakness lay in her choppy English. Fortunately that worked for her in this role.

"My name is Anh. And you are having an affair with my husband," she charged. "He's mine, not yours. He's making a fool out of you. He not love you. He love me. Me he love."

"Liar!" Tiffany cried. "Don's heart is true. He would never lie. Not to me."

Anh cackled. "Fool. He make big fool out of you. Look, I have photograph album of wedding. You want to see it?"

Vicky flinched, caught off guard. "Album? Wait a minute, that doesn't make any sense, Julia," she sneered, mistakenly addressing Julia by her real name instead of her character's.

"Yes, it does," Julia shot back. She displayed natural reserves of power. Holding back was a technique she had picked up from reading books about Marlon Brando and Joan Crawford. Both actors were famous for their ability to turn up the heat when their roles required it. Brando's genius lay in his ability to suggest hidden reservoirs of anger and strength.

She looked at Tiffany. "My album. You know. Lots of pictures. Me in a bright red bridal dress, embroidered with a phoenix and wearing a *khan dong* headdress. Don was wearing a traditional sky blue dress. You mean he not show you the pictures?" Anh exclaimed, toying with her husband's mistress, knowing she was in control.

"I don't believe you," the Tiffany character said weakly. Vicky's halting portrayal made her character seem even weaker.

Anh was laughing. "He may spend nights with you, but he is using you. Then he will come crawling back to me. He'll beg forgiveness. I give it to him. But he must *earn* forgiveness."

"Bitch!" Tiffany shouted. Playing the role hard, Vicky slammed her fist on the table.

At that, both actresses stopped and turned to their acting coach. Igor Steponovich was seated ten feet across from them in a small theatre in New York's Hell's Kitchen. The theatre had a hundred seats. It was reasonably well kept, but the cracking paint on the

44

white ceilings defined a theatrical space that could profit from renovation. Two dozen students sat around him. All were in their early twenties, save for one depressed-looking woman who appeared to be in her early 50s.

They were a mixed bunch. Some, like Julia, were ambitious and aimed to achieve respect and fame as stage-and-screen actors. Mike had raised Julia to understand that success in life was earned through hard work and discipline. Since PH's death, he had lavished love upon her, but the loss of PH had left him depressed.

The saving grace had been Julia. He had poured all of his energy and emotion into making sure that she had everything she needed. Despite the transience of their lives due to his travel schedule, she had grown up to become an A+ student. Julia reciprocated his love. In the loss of PH, they had found mutual strength in one another. That helped each to move forward.

As Julia became a young lady, people remarked that she was the image of her mother. Like PH, she had natural grace and carried herself elegantly. She projected a regal dignity that hid the cauldron of emotions that lay beneath the surface. Her eyes burned with an intensity that brightened every time they laid eyes on her father. Mike called her "Princess." Her father created a zone of safety and security.

Julia had discovered by age ten that she loved theater. Lately she had enrolled in the prestigious acting class over which the famous *auteur*, Igor, presided like a medieval monarch. Now in his late sixties, Igor was a legend in New York. Critics had rated his production of Tennessee William's *A Streetcar Named Desire* the finest play produced on stage in New York during the last decade. One had to watch Laurence Olivier on screen to equal the performances that Igor had elicited from his Broadway-experienced rank of top-tier actors.

45

Between productions the famed producer/director took pride in working as an acting coach. He loved teaching the next generation. He served as muse, guru, role model, and a source of inspiration. All his students felt that he conveyed a dramatic charisma. He brought them alive. He inspired them to look deep within their hearts to understand the characters they portrayed.

Julia revered him. He ignited her passion for the craft. This was especially meaningful to a girl with a mixed heritage, struggling to find her way in American society. Julia knew that when she turned her back, several of her classmates laughed about her accent. The cattiest, and perhaps least talented girls, Vicky, and her best friend Linda, murmured something to the other girls and they all laughed.

Classmates like Vicky and Linda resented and envied Julia's talent. Their shortcomings demanded an excuse. They were desperate to identify a scapegoat, as relief from their insecurities. Julia was an easy target. Her accent alone marked her as different.

Several classmates were also jealous of her luxurious lifestyle. It was one they couldn't miss, since her father made it a point most days of picking her up after class in his luxurious car, or sent his driver to take her back to their Fifth Avenue aerie. For struggling acting students who could barely afford Manhattan rent, it was a sore point, even though Julia never meant to show off her privileges. However, she was picked up after class in a Bentley and she often treated the class to boxes of delicious pastries and little sandwiches made by her family's talented cook.

Julia's father and peers—distinguished, capable business executives or social high-flyers—appreciated hearing different accents. But Julia's peers lacked their sophistication. "Tolerance" did not easily find itself into the vocabulary of Vicky or Linda, or their close friends in the class.

Julia hid her feelings, but girls know how to wound their competition. Julia withdrew into herself. She had resolved to prevail. Still, the snickers and unfair sniping made her feel left out. The ridicule inflamed her insecurity and her feeling that, as a bi-racial female, she would never fit in.

Fortunately, Igor was bigger in heart and soul. His goal was to help the most talented students develop into accomplished actors. Julia had been his first selection, a fact that gave her confidence and made her father and grandmother proud. Igor saw her honesty and integrity. He felt her warmth and generosity.

He also recognized her hard work. He discerned that she had the talent to make it in New York. Frank Sinatra had popularized a song called, "New York, New York". The lyrics proclaimed that if you can make it in here—in *New York*, you can make it anywhere. Igor shared that perspective. New York was the proving ground. He had faith that Julia would make it.

Each year Igor conducted two series of classes. He rigorously interviewed applicants and the competition was fierce. Hundreds applied for two dozen openings. Anxious mothers rang him at home late in the evening pleading with him to give their son or daughter a chance. All of them knew that Igor's blessing meant that casting directors and producers would give an aspiring actor a close look— one that could mean a big break to fame and fortune.

Julia's intention was merely to become the best she could be as an actress and as a singer. She hoped to someday perform in musical theatre productions on Broadway.

Igor ignored pleas for personal favors, even from friends and friends of friends. As a celebrated professional, he chose his students based on potential—those he could mold into artists. In judging how people would do "on the boards," he opted for the most talented. Despite Julia's faltering English, he spotted a certain quality that displayed a depth of honesty and the ability to reach deep down to reveal truth.

Julia beamed when Igor promised that he would help unlock her talent. "You could be a star, Julia," he advised, "but you'll have to keep applying yourself. Acting is a craft. People study it for years and only the lucky few make it. Luck and talent are the winning combination, but hard work can make the difference. Your accent presents an obstacle. I say that because I have to be honest."

"How bad a problem is it?" Julia worried.

He gave a reassuring smile. "You can do it, Julia. The important thing is to believe in yourself. Forget the jealousy that you arouse. It happens because you can do things they can only imagine."

"Why?" Julia had asked. "I try to be honest with people."

"You have a good heart. It is one of your nice qualities." Igor had looked at her with a serious expression. "Life is like that. Your competitors see that you speak and look different. Yet you will best them for acting roles because you are gifted in ways they are not. Staying the course demands faith—deep faith, in yourself, in your family, in me. Do you have that faith?"

Julia's inability to attain full fluency in English bothered her more now than it always had. "Nobody works harder than me," she said. *"Nobody."* She paused. "And yes, I have faith." Her gaze was unwavering.

"I know," Igor said, smiling at the exotic young woman. "I can see the resolution in your face. Your eyes reveal truth. I am honored to have you among my students."

The acting classes provided happy experiences. Still, her mother's tragic death haunted her. Julia was now twenty-three. Too often during the night, images of the car crash flashed back and woke her, and she had sat up, screaming "No!"

At Igor's request, Vicky and Julia repeated their scene about Anh and Tiffany for a second time. When they finished, their performances elicited polite applause. Igor stood up as he joined in the applause. He looked at the class and then at Julia and Vicky and enthusiastically complimented his two students. "Bravo, Bravo!" he exclaimed. He looked at Julia. "Julia, you are improving rapidly." From the back rows, two of Julia's classmates snickered, but stopped their mockery as Igor shot them a stern look. He turned back to Julia with a broad smile.

Julia smiled shyly and bowed. "Thank you, Igor," she said, addressing him by his first name as he had instructed his students to do. As he had explained, theatre was an intimate experience, and personal relationships required dispensing with formality.

Igor turned to Vicky and graced her with his smile. As always, he was encouraging. "And you, my dear. Your performance is becoming measured and poignant." Vicky grinned, warmed by his praise, even though she had no idea what he meant. She was cocky and used to praise. Indeed she had come to expect it. People said gentlemen preferred blondes. She was a poster child for that precept. Somehow her attractive All-American-Girl appearance clouded the fact that behind the rows of polished white teeth and expensive wardrobe, she was a viper.

"Thank You, Igor!" Vicky replied. Her right hand still tightly gripped the phone she had used as a prop, reflecting the residue of emotion from her role as a woman betrayed.

Igor stood and turned to the students. "Julia and Vicky have studied hard. I thought they did an excellent job and demonstrated good focus. Class, focus is key. It's about concentration. It requires you to engage with your characters so that we believe in them. Audiences have no wish to watch cardboard cut-out figures prance about the stage. They want to feel that the characters are experiencing some-thing *real*. They want to empathize. Project genuine feeling and the audience will experience it with you." He paused to be sure they were taking it all in, then continued, "When Laurence Olivier played Hamlet, audiences identified with his character. Father-son, daugh-ter-father, mother-father relationships go to the essence of drama. So do husband-wife relationships. That's what Julia and Vicky were showing us. I applaud their efforts."

He turned to the two actresses. Igor glanced back at the other students. They took their cue and applauded. The two young women bowed in acknowledgement. Igor advised the class that encouraging one another and offering support was a major lesson. Every produc-tion, amateur or professional, required a team effort—whether they had the lead or a supporting role.

Julia carefully observed the reactions of her classmates. She was always careful to praise her classmates when they did well. She cheered them on. Never did she show jealousy. Only Jason Rodri-guez, the class hunk, stood apart. He was a tall, lanky, square-jawed and handsome guy in his mid-twenties with a friendly face and a shock of unruly dark hair. Jason appreciated Julia and made his feel-ings clear to everyone else. He knew how talented Julia was, but what he especially liked was her warmth and sincerity.

They had become fast friends. Jason loved to tease Julia. Indeed, rather than cut her any slack about her accent, he liked to gently joke with her about it. Julia relished his gentle mirth, which was never mean-spirited. In Jason she found one American who welcomed her. Jason was a man her father would respect. He had the right values. He listened when she spoke. He treated her as an equal. She consid-ered Jason's presence in the class a gift of good fortune.

Julia had proven an astute judge of others. Their jealousy inspired contempt. If they envied her rich and handsome father, who called her his Princess, and picked her up in his chauffeured car after class, their reactions were their problem. Still, she felt like she was standing on the wrong side of the glass. Over and over she asked herself: *Why am I an outsider?* She blamed her woes on her poor English and the fact that she looked different from other Americans.

Julia cast an eye at Vicky and prepared to walk over and compliment her fellow aspirant. Noticing Julia looking in her direction, Vicky turned, her body language sending a clear message: *stay away.* At the same time Vicky continued to look eagerly at Igor, hoping for another compliment. Igor caught what had happened. He walked over to Julia and gave her a hug. Vicky grimaced.

A few minutes later she put on her coat and got ready to meet her father, who had texted that he would be waiting outside in the back seat of their chauffeured Lincoln Town Car. Buoyed by Igor's compliments, she felt great about herself. *I better get a move on*, she thought. Papa's waiting.

As she moved towards the door, Jason caught up with her. He held the door open for her. "Great job, Julia," he said. "Let me walk you out."

The other girls had stopped to watch this scene play out. "Get her," one of the others whispered to Vicky, "You carried the scene and she cops the class hottie." They scoffed, then burst out laughing. Fortunately Julia was already out the door and had jumped into the back seat next to her father. Today, Mike is a wealthy American, living a life of privilege, traveling by his private jet , staying at five-star hotels. The owner of a luxurious condominium penthouse in New York and a weekend mansion in the country, he seemed to have it all. Unfortunately, Phuong Ha is not alive to enjoy these material things. Since the death of his beloved wife sixteen years ago, Mike has become more mindful of car safety. Mike had chosen his driver carefully. Max doubled as chauffeur and bodyguard. He had gained his experience serving in the Israeli army.

Jason watched the car drive away. He was developing an interest in Julia, and wished she would consider going out with him. They were not paired as acting partners. Despite playing opposite Vicky today, more regularly Igor had paired her with Bethany, while assigning Jason to Vicky, who was needy and pushy. Vicky had made overtures to him, but he wasn't interested. Perhaps he could persuade Igor to make a change. He wanted to know Julia better. *Such a magnificent creature!* He hoped she didn't have a secret boyfriend. That would be a shame. She wasn't like those self-centered bitches that he had met too often in the theatre: people who put themselves and their ambitions ahead of all else.

He wanted to spend more time in Julia's company. What man in his right mind wouldn't?

Chapter Five

In the large dressing room of their Hamptons home, Mike Chamonix straightened his foulard tie and smoothed down the front of his smart navy-blue, pin-striped suit, tailored for him by Poole & Co. He looked distinguished in the suit, with a confident air. Anybody who dealt with him in business knew that he came well prepared. He was a shrewd negotiator, but his idea of success entailed seeking a win-win for both parties. It was a quality that Julia loved about him. Her father was all things: a champion in his professional field, a caring and loving father at home, her constant companion, and the rock that formed the foundation of her life.

As Mike was about to leave his bedroom, he found Julia in the hallway caressing the tiny pearls on her mother's Ivory wedding dress. It was not the one she had worn that day in the lush gardens in Ho Chi Minh City. PH had worn a more traditional Vietnamese wedding costume then. This was the wedding dress that PH had worn for the lavish wedding held later on in New York for Mike's American friends.

For the more traditional wedding for their family and friends in Vietnam, her bridal gown had been a deep crimson red and embroidered with gold thread. Many Vietnamese brides choose the national costume, *ao dai*, modeled after the Nguyen Dynasty court ladies. It is a long silk tunic that is worn over pants. A circular headdress, the *khan dong*, completes the look. Many Vietnamese brides chose red, a color thought to bring a couple good luck.

Julia loved both of her mother's gowns, which had acquired an iconic status in her family. But her favorite remained the ivory one sprinkled with delicate pearls. Queen Victoria had started that fashion in 1840, in her wedding to Prince Albert. The dress was a tangible expression of the warmth and generosity in her heart. It was her talisman, a vision of her mother reassuring her each day.

As Julia's fingertips graced the bodice of her mother's gown she was unaware of her father watching her. Looking at her now, he was startled to realize that, physically, Julia seemed a replica of PH.

Julia knew no one could substitute for her mother. No-one could occupy that role. She also knew that she bore an uncanny resemblance to PH. She hoped her father would see her that. Something inside her wanted more from him, but she knew it was not healthy to desire her father sexually, so she tried to deny her emerging passionate urges. Sometimes in the dark of night, she gave in to her secret passion and imagined that she was her mother. She envisioned herself in her mother's wedding gown, dripping in jewels, wearing her hair up in a French Roll, kissing Mike.

She suddenly noticed she was not alone. "Oh! Father!" Julia flushed, jolted to reality.

"I'm sorry. I was just so stunned. I didn't realize until now that you have grown to look exactly like your mother when she wore this incredible gown," he smiled, kissing the top of her head.

"Do you really think I'm as beautiful as my mother?" Julia beamed.

"Absolutely. Any man would be lucky to have you," he said.

Any man? She thought to herself with a dreamy sigh.

As Mike moved into the kitchen, Julia hung back and regarded the dress. Touching its silky fabric enlivened her. It was as if her mother's spirit was entwined with hers.

She had touched it often—always glancing at the large portrait of her parents taken the day of their New York wedding. In one vision, Julia saw herself in the gown, dancing with Mike around

54

the parquet floor of a fancy ballroom, her father's arm possessively around her waist, gazing with passion into her eyes.

Anxious to foster a cosmopolitan outlook, Mike had advised one evening: "I want you to meet people from all over the world. The more different types of people you meet, the more easily you will make new friends." They had been dressing to meet some Parisian bankers at the famed brasserie, La Coupole, on Montparnasse Avenue, famous for its raw oysters, steak fritte, and their wildly popular floating island dessert.

Julia reveled in these trips. Always, Mike treated her as an adult, as did his clients. She charmed them, and they respected Mike for including his Julia in these outings. They made her feel special. Of course he missed PH, but having her at his side was almost like having his wife there. Mike found satisfaction in the fact that Julia loved being with him. It deepened their love. Indeed, her presence was so ubiquitous that she knew that neither she nor Mike could imagine spending time alone. She didn't just love her father, she adored him. The reverence she held for him wove a spiritual bond of love that had grown stronger over time. She would honor her mother's memory by living the life she never got to live.

Reaching the age of fifteen, an inescapable sensibility had taken root. Even if Julia was unable to fully understand it, she had fallen deeply in love with her father.

****

Julia hummed as she entered the kitchen and her father handed her a cup of lemon tea. "Are you doing anything special today, father?" Julia asked, as she reached out to straighten his tie, and smooth down the shoulders of his jacket. They needed no further straightening, but it felt good to touch him. She looked at him with bright eyes and hope in her expression. Mike returned the smile and gave her shoulder a squeeze.

"Of course I'm doing something special, Princess," he laughed. "I do it every day. I'm thinking of you. I'm taking pride in my beautiful daughter."

"I love you, too," Julia said.

Mike checked himself in the full length mirror and was pleased with his reflection. His voice brimmed with anticipation. "By the way, I have exciting news."

"Tell me," Julia said.

He cocked one brow, looked her straight in the face, and stated, "I've managed to acquire a painting by Marc Chagall."

"Who?" she wondered. "Is he a family friend?"

He chuckled. "We've never met. Nor will we. He's dead."

"Guess there's a lot I don't know about art," Julia said, a bit embarrassed.

"Don't be silly, honey. No one can know everything about everything. Marc Chagall worked in France. His paintings cost a lot of money today, and they're difficult to get hold of. A friend managed to snag one from an art dealer in London."

Julia looked around the room. An oil painting by Picasso, done in his cubic period, graced one wall. She rubbed her chin. "Don't we already have plenty of paintings?" Julia mused. "You're buying another one?"

"Always room for another addition," Mike nodded. "This one will fill just the right wall space near the front door."

Mike walked over to her and kissed her on her cheek. "We'll put a plaque beneath the Chagall. It will read: *Acquired for Julia*." She turned to him and he leaned forward. "What do you think?"

Julia shrugged. "Maybe."

"*Maybe?*" Mike frowned. "Darling, Google him." He gave her a sly look. "Of course, he didn't have *your* artistic ability, but he was pretty good." She laughed affectionately. "I think this work will pay tribute to a wonderful young lady." He pointed to her comically. "That would be you."

She nodded cheerfully. "Come, father, breakfast has been prepared, and grandmother is waiting in the dining room."

They were in their weekend home, an expansive modern mansion in an exclusive Westchester suburb, just outside Manhattan. Designed by Jude Horwith, a discipline of the famed architect Frank Lloyd Wright, the home resembled Wright's famous Crystal Bridges residence with 14-foot floor-to-ceiling glass plate windows that looked over an open floor plan with grey tiled floors. It was a perfect showcase for both modern art and antique eighteenth century English furniture. It was sleek but warm, and though austere in its look somehow was still inviting and intimate.

They reached the ornate dining room with its long mahogany table, where Julia's grandmother, Van, was pouring tea. Van had asked the cook to lay out a light breakfast of fresh muffins and scones, jam, and creamy butter, along with bowls of fresh fruit. Julia stepped to the Nespresso coffee machine, turned it on, inserted a Roma capsule and made her father a single-shot espresso. She served it to him proudly. "For you, papa!"

"Thank you, Princess," Mike exclaimed. He took a sip. "Umm. Perfect." He gave her a wink.

"You like?" Julia laughed.

"The best!" Mike said. "Like you."

"Speak proper English, Julia," her grandmother said. Van, though just past 70 years of age, had the posture and energy of someone younger. She was slender and elegant, with long grey hair and a yellow dress adorned with a flower pattern. She wore a thin gold necklace to accent the dress, and beautiful low heeled shoes. "It is important that you speak properly."

"I try," Julia said, hesitantly. "I try hard."

"Good morning, Van," Mike said, "Don't you look lovely, this morning. Ahh! Ahh! But then you do every morning. "He kissed her on the cheek and she gracefully bowed her head. He found her to be a wise and sensible woman, and appreciated her helping him raise Julia.

"Good morning to you as well," she said.

"Julia's language skills are improving every week. I can see it. I can feel it," Mike said. Mike took care to avoid insincerely flattering Julia. He knew she could spot a false note. Nothing got past Van.

"Mike," she stated, looking from him to her granddaughter, "Julia must do this perfectly. She must speak English well to get ahead, especially in the performing arts. Otherwise, the only roles open to her will be for her Asian half. She has the potential to become a star. That requires hard work. You will not let her off the hook."

Mike nodded. Van was correct. Julia winced, well aware that not speaking English fluently would not do.

Mike rose to her defense. "She will get there Van." He cast a sideways look at Julia, then turned back to Van. "Julia is never going to fail. She's got my blood—and yours. Like the song says, she can climb any mountain."

"Good!" Van declared approvingly. She stared straight into Julia's eyes. "I expect nothing less." Her eyes danced as she looked back at Mike. "By the way, be sure you come home tonight in time for dinner. Julia and I are making your favorite meal—Vietnamese egg rolls."

58

"Egg rolls? Really?" Mike said, salivating. He loved the way Van and Julia prepared dishes. Although Americans tended to view egg rolls as a routine appetizer in restaurants, properly done they were works of art that gourmets savored. He finished his espresso.

Julia was smiling brightly. "We make them just for you."

Mike feigned shock. "Me? Just for me?"

"Yes," Julia said, pointing her finger at him for emphasis. "You!"

"Well then I better get off to work so I can be home in time," he answered. He grabbed his coat.

Van touched his arm. "One minute before you go," she said. She walked to a small Sheraton table on which she had a small pile of stacked mail, picked up a letter and held it out. "The foundation sent this. They're hoping Julia can come to Ho Chi Minh City for the opening of a new orphanage there. Helping people is part of Julia's heritage—and matters so much to the people of Vietnam. It's different from America. We don't have Social Security or safety nets. Families take care of themselves—and we help strangers like they are our neighbors."

"When is it?" Mike asked. The news excited him as much as it had Van and Julia.

"In four months," Van said. Handing him the letter, she stood up erectly. Van was a proud woman and a strong person who was at peace with herself. That quality inspired tranquility within the family and gave Julia a sense of security. She loved her grandmother, who always took care to show Julia her love. One of her secrets for bringing joy to Julia and Mike lay in her gift for creating cuisine. When she was younger, Van had attended a cooking school in Ho Chi Minh City. Except that she was devoted to family, which always came first, she could have been the chef in a top-tier restaurant. She loved surprising them with new Vietnamese dishes.

Van felt strongly about the foundation that Phuong Ha had originated, and any time an event occurred that provided her with an opportunity to support it, she became a vocal advocate.

Mike scanned the letter, then looked at Julia. "So what's the verdict? You up for a 21-hour flight back home to Vietnam?"

"You bet!" Julia squealed!

Mike clasped his daughter's hands. "Want to know what I think?"

"What?" she asked, waiting for what she hoped he would say.

"I think you and your grandmother ought to book tickets for the three of us. First class."

Julia exhaled. "Yes, yes, yes!"

A wan smile crossed Van's face. "First class!" Her manner was airy. "Mike, you do know how to take care of your family."

"Family comes first," Mike said.

"Be home for dinner," Julia repeated. "We eat at 8:00 sharp." She paused, pleased that she could deliver the English colloquialism without missing a beat.

"Sharp!" Mike repeated. "I'm in." He blew them kisses and walked out the door.

Chapter Six

The Gallery *Coburn* stood out as a modern temple well designed to display major artistic achievements. It's curator, Jennifer Coburn, was a tall, lanky woman in her early thirties, with high cheekbones, emerald green eyes, and natural poise. Her streaked blonde hair, in a short, stylish bob, framed her angular face. She was striking rather than conventionally pretty, with strong features. Her boyish figure ensconced in a Prada tailored dress, marked a self-confident woman who knew her business and excelled at pleasing a select clientele.

Jennifer had deliberately situated the gallery in a cast-iron building on Grand Street at the corner of Lafayette in Lower Manhattan's "South of Houston district," commonly known as "SoHo." The name drew its reference not only from its proximity to Houston Street, but also from London's SoHo district.

The gallery was an expression of Jennifer: elegant, iconic, a woman who threw her heart and soul into her work. Artists she represented loved her. They knew she stood four-square behind their art and worked tirelessly to sell it. Even more important, she had a track record of sustained success. When she took on a client, they knew they were getting the best.

The gallery featured 30-foot tall ceilings with broad spaces and natural light that showed the artwork off to it's best advantage. In-demand artists at the highest end, like Jeff Koons, Jasper Johns, and David Hammons preferred Tony galleries on West 57th or Madison Avenue. But the next generation loved the bohemian chic that defined SoHo. The Villa Design Group, Duda Bador, and Cornelia

Baltes, exemplified the caliber of gifted artists whom Jennifer courted. She had also earned a reputation as a tough negotiator in the international market for Impressionists, Post-Impressions, Surrealists, and Abstract Expressionists such as Jackson Pollack. Her favorite was Andy Warhol.

Warhol's trademark white-blond hair—which was actually a wig—and thick glasses defined his look as much as his art. The leading figure in the pop art visual art movement, he had operated from a studio he called The Factory. The Factory drew Hollywood celebrities, East Coast intellectuals, playwrights like Tennessee Williams, bohemians, and the very wealthy. Perhaps Warhol's most famous work turned iconic objects such as electric chairs and Campbell's Soup Cans into art. His silk screen portraits were legendary, featuring the faces of Marilyn Monroe, Elizabeth Taylor, Elvis Presley, and Muhammad Ali, among many other notables.

Ironically, a tongue-in-cheek quality defined Warhol's approach, as if he were mocking the pretense that surrounded his hype. Despite charging $50,000 for silk-screens, his marketing gimmick was eerily simple. Potential clients were invited to The Factory for lunch. The draw was celebrity, not the food. One might encounter famous people, but lunch consisted of chicken salad or ham sandwiches from a nearby deli. Despite the cutting-edge tone of his public face, privately Warhol was a classicist. His own home was packed with museum-quality antique furniture and bric-a-brac.

After his death, Warhol's paintings escalated in value. Mike had desperately wanted one for his offices in Rockefeller Plaza. Actually, the Chagall was originally intended for the offices as well, but he would keep this morning's promise to Julia.

Mike strode into the gallery, pausing to admire a De Kooning that Jennifer was selling on consignment. He noticed a couple at the other end of the gallery gazing at a Helen Frankenthaler, then looked across to Jennifer.

She was engaged in an intense conversation with a tall, bespectacled man in a grey suit and silk burgundy shirt who spoke in the kind of arch accent favored by theatrical stars in the 1930's—and by art dealers on the Upper East Side. He was typical of the smart, high-end collectors with whom Jennifer had forged a strong business relationship. Mike respected Jennifer for her superb taste, her extensive knowledge of modern art, and her ability to network among major collectors. Noticing Mike, Jennifer gave him a big smile, held up her hand and wiggled five fingers to indicate she would try to be with him shortly. She then returned to her conversation.

Mike strolled around the gallery, taking in the exhibition of work by the Harlem-born Tschabalala Self that celebrated the complex sexiness of her work. Collectors called her style the "anti-Picasso." There was also a new collection by Torey Thornton, known for his buoyant paintings: abstracted forms resembling parking lots, amoebas and gigantic flowers floating among one another.

Finally the first couple left and, to Mike's relief, Jennifer shook hands with the other man and engaged with him only briefly. The man bowed stiffly and left, a pleased expression on his face.

Mike and Jennifer stepped close to one another and exchanged a warm handshake. He held her hand a moment longer than necessary and gave her an admiring look. "So, did you make a big sale?" Jennifer smiled and replied in her cultured voice. "Maybe. He's about 90% of the way there for the de Kooning." She nodded towards a colorful abstract expressionist painting with broad brushstrokes and vivid colors that hung near the front of the gallery.

"I see. And what are you asking for that little gem?" He cast an eye towards it. It was about 48 inches by 50 inches. His painting, entitled *Woman III*, had sold not long before for $137.5 million.

She responded coyly. "Oh, I don't think that's a good choice. For you—or him."

"Well, as for me, I expect a Christmas gift."

"That would be Godiva," she said, knowing his fondness for chocolate.

"I only do Belgium. Corne Port Royal, please."

"No wonder you like the de Kooning. We're going to have to put you on a budget."

"Not for chocolate," he teased. "Belvas is fine. Especially the Fairtrade truffles and pralines."

She laughed and their eyes met. Ever since meeting, they had felt a mutual attraction. The gallery was now empty and he drew her to him and kissed her lightly. She smiled and embraced him. They enjoyed a long, languid kiss. He drew back, lifting an eyebrow flirtatiously. "Now that's what I call a work of art."

"Don't get fresh with me, buddy," she shot back. "This gallery trades at the high end."

He responded by kissing her again, their tongues meshed hungrily with a potency that took his breath away. Mike could feel his pulse race, but stifled his desire. *Later*, he thought.

"Did anyone caution you that such behavior qualifies as PDA - a public display of affection?" she asked with a straight face, trying to lighten the mood and slow down her own heartbeat. He was *such* an attractive man. In her mind, Mike was the catch of the century.

"I probably should have done time in a home for delinquents," he countered.

"Not too late," she teased.

"I have a plan," he said.

"Oh?"

"Good plan. No, a great plan."

"I trust it includes dinner at Il Bruggio."

"You know it. But dessert's special."

She looked at him seductively. "Tell me more."

"Doesn't lend itself to the discursive arts," he explained. Gazing at her, he was filled with longing and desire. It had been a long time. Not that he hadn't slept with a few women. But no one thus far had captured his respect—or his heart. For the first time since his wife's death, he felt something more than lust. Jennifer had potential.

She drew a breath, and gave his hand a squeeze. "Come here," she said. "I have something to show you." She led him to her office, just off the gallery floor. It had a severely modern décor, and her large glass desk was stacked with papers. On one wall, taking it over completely, was an oil by Umberto Boccioni entitled *The Metropolis Rises*. Boccioni was a major futurist who had abandoned naturalism to articulate technology through electrified paint handling. It was her favorite piece of art.

Entering the office, which ensured privacy from public view, they kissed again, then she pushed him away playfully. "I have a surprise."

"Show me," he said, his eyes widening in anticipation.

She stepped to a table and held up a large, heavy package wrapped in brown paper. "Perhaps you might take a gander at this," she said.

"What is that?" he said, like a child opening his most wanted Christmas gift.

"See for yourself. If it doesn't meet your taste, I know some other folks dying to grab it—at twice what you'll pay."

"I'm getting only 50% off?"

"Other nice things come with it—Package deal," she flirted.

He made a great show of unwrapping the package. The contents—the Chagall he had long coveted—took his breath away. It was astonishing. Art historian Jean Leymarie had observed that Chagall began his career thinking of art as "emerging from the internal being outward, from the seen object to the psychic outpouring." Paris intoxicated Chagall. A stroll through the French capital exhilarated him and inspired his surrealist style. But the painting that Mike held, depicting a circus, measured up to Chagall's aspiration to create works that inspired happiness and instinctive compassion. The painting featured musicians—a figurative theme in much of his work. Chagall himself had said, as one critic reported, "that clowns and acrobats always resembled figures in religious paintings." Chagall had further explained that their makeup and facial expressions touched him.

Mike held up the painting and stared at it for two minutes without speaking. Then he drew a breath. He looked at Jennifer. "It's done? The Chagall's mine?"

Her eyes sparkled. "All yours. And for exactly what you wanted to pay."

"Decourves came down?" He meant the London collector who was offering the painting for private sale.

She shrugged. "We drank a lot of tea together. I offered to wire the money this afternoon. Smart move, you opening the escrow account and giving me power of attorney to wire it. Nothing like cold cash to move a deal."

"You are one hell of a closer, my dear."

"Yes, I am," she acknowledged. "And don't you forget it. By the way, I'm hungry."

"Okay off we go. By the way, let me ask you again: What are you planning to have for dessert?" he asked.

"You're a gentleman with a great imagination. You get two guesses. Both of them are correct."

Chapter Seven

Julia's grandmother, Van, Phuong Ha's lovely and accomplished mother, had made her famous Vietnamese egg rolls for Phuong Ha's wedding to Mike. In Van's mind, wonderful food was an expression of love and joy. She lacked nothing being in charge of the kitchen.

The great Vietnamese chefs take pride in creating their own recipes. Van had a genius for creating certain dishes. She was original in her approach, and her dishes stood out. Guests showed their appreciation by asking for seconds.

Julia took her cue from her grandmother. Just as she wanted to be more like her mother, Julia wanted to emulate Van, her role model as a great humanitarian and a woman of deep wisdom.

The egg rolls represented one of Van's best recipes. Van coyly refused to divulge the secret to why her egg rolls were the best. But it was common knowledge that four key elements make the finest egg rolls: Taro root, which has a consistency like a potato; minced pork or dried black fungus; cellophane noodles, and the rice wrappers. Julia's favorite was Spring Home TY, which Asian grocery stores in America sell. A lot of care goes into creating this delicacy. Rolling them is important, using egg whites as glue for the egg roll. After preparation, they are fried.

One day, as Van was teaching Julia, who listened carefully anytime her grandmother spoke, her grandmother made a point that one must never confuse the Vietnamese version with Chinese egg rolls. As she explained, the Chinese wrap theirs in a wheat base wrapper. The textural differences are dramatic. Rice paper roll is crispy, bubbly, and chewy. Wheat wrappers fail to achieve the golden brown color that makes the Vietnamese version so alluring. When rice paper hits the hot oil, it bubbles up and blisters. Both contain a variety of chopped vegetables. Van and Julia were making theirs with chopped vegetables and chicken. They had selected wood ear mushrooms and thread noodles, as well as shredded jicama, taro, and bean sprouts.

Grandmother and granddaughter worked hard together that afternoon. They were a team. They shared in all aspects of preparation for the egg rolls. They were going all out to make Mike happy. They knew how much he *loved* the egg rolls. He had cancelled or postponed business meetings in Manhattan to get home in time for dinner every time they made them.

More often, they let him know in the morning when they planned to make them. There was no choice. It was a matter of scheduling. Mike was a notorious workaholic. Although a loving parent at home, he tended to arrive at his office early and work into the evening. When he worked late, Mike was always careful to call Julia and when he had to cancel a dinner he always made a point of coming up with something special they could do together to make up for his absence. It might be something small, such as where he might take Julia and Van to dinner in the next few days, or what show on Broadway they might like to see so he could get the tickets.

Julia respected how hard Mike worked, and knew that the high-powered business tycoons he did business with in New York, Paris, London, Rome, and Tokyo respected him for it. "Americans like to say 'the early bird gets the worm.' It's a cliché but it epitomizes the importance of hard work. Hard work is how you win the big ones." Miles always said.

Julia had heeded his advice. It was why she prepared so diligently for her theater classes. Everyone wanted to impress Igor—and with good reason. Igor had *connections*. He knew everybody. He could open doors that the world closed to outsiders. Igor was a supportive, encouraging mentor. Still, he placed a condition on his generosity. He warned that acting was a craft as much as an art. It drained emotions. It could be physically stressful. So when her father dispensed advice to Julia on the need for discipline—especially as she worked to speak English more fluently—she heeded his counsel.

Van reminded Julia that her grandfather—her late husband—had achieved his success as the owner of several clothing stores in Vietnam through the same philosophy. *Bat ca hai tay*, she liked to say. *You catch fish with two hands*. In other words—*apply yourself*.

Van was a reservoir of Vietnamese proverbs. Her most important one, her mantra, was *Co cong mai sat co ngay nen kim: Persevere and never fear*. Because she had fought to master English and develop her acting craft, Julia realized the truth in that wisdom. It worked for acting. It also worked as she helped to prepare egg rolls.

By now the evening light had faded and darkness was descending. Julia was growing impatient. She looked up at the silver wall clock mounted on the kitchen wall. A shadow crossed her face. "Grandma, clock say 7:15. When is papa coming home?"

Van gave Julia a benevolent smile. "Your father works very hard, Julia. We said dinner was at 8:00, remember?"

Julia folded her arms defiantly and her tone was sharp. "I hope he is on time. Egg rolls are best when served immediately, right after they are ready. They will get soggy if he is late and will be no good at all!" She did not mean to sound harsh about her father. Still, she and Van had toiled for him, she expected the same consideration. It was not like Mike to arrive late for dinner without calling ahead, and when he did do that, there was good reason.

But 8:00 arrived and then 8:30. The hands of the clock continued to move with no sign of Mike. "Grandma," Julia said, "he's late." Julia was confused. Where was papa? If work delayed him, why had he not called? This was unusual, to say the least. She walked to the living room, reached into her Hermes textured Togo calfskin leather Birkin 35 Rouge handbag with solid gold hardware and pulled out her iPhone. She hit the phone's keyboard and heard it ringing through to Mike's cell. Moments later a cheerful voice answered: "Hi! It's Mike!" His cadence was so natural she fell for it every time.

"Papa!" she cried, but then the voice went on to say "Please leave your name and I'll get back to you very shortly."

Fuming, she practically barked into the phone. "Father, it's Julia. The egg rolls are ready. They are getting cold. We worked for hours. We did this for *you*. Where are you?" She disconnected. She turned to see Van watching her.

"Voice mail?" Van asked.

Julia nodded. Her voice carried loud and clear across the open space of the living room as her face darkened. "You think papa is all right? What if he was in an accident?" Saying the words caused her body to shudder. The awful image of her mother's death haunted her every day. The concept that her father might meet the same fate frightened her. In some ways, Julia was a fatalist. People should work hard, yes. But sometimes fate decided things for you, and there wasn't anything you could do about it.

There was a momentary silence, then Van came to Julia and clasped her. "Do not worry about your father. I am sure he is just in meetings that ran overtime and he couldn't call. Everything will be fine."

"You promise?" Julia said, a question marking her tone, as if reassurance could never achieve the certainty that would put her mind at ease.

"Promise," Van said, kissing Julia lightly on the head.

"Well, if you say so." She cast an eye towards the kitchen. "But the egg rolls are getting cold." Almost always the thought of her father enlivened her spirits. His failure to show this evening dampened them.

"They can easily be warmed," Van said. "He will enjoy them no matter what time he gets home."

Van's encouragement reassured Julia. For the next hour, they cleaned the kitchen and set the table for three. But the good cheer elapsed as 10:00 arrived. Impatiently, Julia called Mike again. Each time her finger hit the speed dial for his cell number on her iPhone, her anticipation grew. Tonight, though, there was only disappointment. Again and again she received Mike's voicemail.

"Something is not right," Julia said irritably. This time there wasn't much that Van could say. It was unlike him. She would never acknowledge it, but she also began to harbor fears. *Could the gods truly be that cruel? Would they really visit a second tragedy upon the family?* A strong woman, Van forced the thought from her mind. She remained uncharacteristically silent.

Finally Julia sat down and rested her chin on her hands. A small tear formed in one corner of her eye. "Papa, why you do this?" she said out loud in a plaintively, almost childlike voice.

Van placed plates of egg rolls on the table for each of them. "Eat, child. Food restores the spirits." She helped herself to a bite and her face brightened. "Yes, this is what we call *egg rolls*." She shrugged. "We must take the positive view. We get to enjoy them while they are fresh. The one who loses out tonight is Mike. He will be sorry."

Julia's expression conveyed no doubt that she intended to drive home the message to her father when he finally showed up. Had he no consideration for the effort they had made to please him? With her appetite gone, she pushed herself away from the table, excused herself, and went to her bedroom. This had not been a good night. Julia felt acutely let down by Mike. Above all, his behavior confused her.

****

Mike was with Jennifer at her apartment. She had an alluring way about her. He liked the way she talked, the way she dressed, the smooth way that she handled herself. Jennifer had a perfectly-proportioned body with narrow hips, flat stomach and small but soft, well-rounded breasts. Mike had appointed himself the role of explorer. He intended to investigate every nook and cranny. Mike instinctively gathered her into his arms and carried her to the bedroom, where they made love well into the night. The egg rolls never once crossed Mike's mind.

****

In their Westchester mansion, Julia restlessly tossed and turned, unable to sleep. The stroke of midnight chimed on her hand-crafted Swiss bedroom clock. She loved the sound of the bells and chimes from Westminster Cathedral in London. There was something poetic and comforting about the stately sound of the gongs marking time. Tonight, though, time seemed to tick on as she counted the minutes.

After she left her grandmother, Julia had changed into a red satin negligee and sat up in bed, trying to study some of the plays Igor had assigned the class to read. Concentration had proved futile. She kept worrying about her father. She loved him so deeply that his absence stung further. She felt herself lost on an out-of-control emotional roller coaster. One moment she was on the verge of tears, the next she gripped her hands together in anger. She drummed her fingers on the hardcover of the book that contained the *Collected Works of William Shakespeare.*

Giving up on reading, Julie turned off the lamp beside her bed and sank back into her fluffy down Pratesi pillows, the most stylish Italian linens to pamper royalty across the world. Mike treated his daughter like a princess and both of her bedrooms—the one here and the one in their penthouse in Manhattan—were indeed, fashionably decorated in a manner suitable for royalty. None of that comforted Julia right now though. All she could think about was her father lying dead somewhere. Why else would he have failed to call?

Fidgeting and worried, she recalled an incident from her childhood. She was a young girl again, perhaps four, the year before her mother died in the car crash, when she had awakened in the middle of the night. She had been laying in her bed, lightly dozing, when the insistent sound of cries and moans wafted down the hall. Was somebody hurting mama? Getting up, she put on her slippers and stealthily walked towards her parent's bedroom. The door was slightly ajar. From where she stood in the hallway, she could see her father's naked body mounted on top of her mother, his sweaty back was rhythmically rising and thrusting forward into her mother.

Every time he moved forward, his mother let out a cry of pleasure. Julia's eyes grew wide recalling how her father feverishly kissed PH's breasts and how her long, smooth legs wrapped around him in an intense erotic embrace. They were groping each other in a tangled passionate web of intense stroking and kissing that seemed to last forever, becoming more frantic as their moans and cries grew faster and louder until they finally collapsed into each other's arms, panting and relieved. Both her mother's cries and her father's deep moans rang in her ears for a long time, even as she quietly returned to her own room. That memory had always stayed with her.

She straightened her legs and gently spread them apart. She allowed her right hand to slide down her body, caressing the inside of her thigh lightly, before slipping her probing fingers beneath the lacy band of her now soaked underpants, then moved a finger into the dark mound of soft fine pubic hair to find her throbbing lips. She envisioned Mike's exposed buttocks forcefully plunging into her mother, and how she had cried out in ecstasy upon reaching climax.

Julia caressed her lips slowly and gently at first before curiously finding her clitoris. She imagined she was Phuong Ha making love to Mike. The vision of his hard body pounding into hers brought her to new heights.

A few minutes later she felt her body start to quiver, and perspire as she sped up her stroking, involuntarily emitting a soft moan. Instinctively she slipped her middle finger deep inside her vagina, plunging it feverishly in and out, imagining it was Mike who was pleasing her with such potent desire. Her body convulsed wildly as she arched her back off the bed; her clitoris pulsated in several waves as she came over and over again. She collapsed against the soft pillow, breathing deeply and looked at the clock.

Her father was her soul mate, and a tear formed in the corner of her eye at that thought while she caught her breath. Now Mike was daddy again, not her phantom lover, and her last thought, as she drifted off to sleep, was to hope he was safe and thinking of her as well wherever he was.

Chapter Eight

Waking up the next morning, Mike reached for his iPhone lying on the night table next to him. As he grabbed it, he felt Jennifer lazily stir and then become fully awake. He looked over at her with a satisfied smile.

"Hi," he said.

"Hi yourself," she returned his smile.

He put down the phone and they embraced and kissed.

"That was nice last night," she said. "You're very, very good."

"You're an Amazon," he observed.

"Write that down and don't forget it." She noticed his phone. "Business this early?"

Mike picked up the phone and realized he had turned the phone to mute. He checked his recent calls and saw that Julia had left three voicemail messages amid seven attempts. He felt a fleeting moment of guilt. This was the first time in his life he had failed to let his daughter know when he wasn't coming home. He checked the time and saw that it was already 8:00 a.m. The realization sent a shock through his body. He loved and adored Julia, and knew she would be disappointed. He hated letting Julia down. She had high expectations and he did his best to meet them so it was no wonder that a side of him felt a twinge of guilt for not calling her.

"Something wrong?" Jennifer asked.

"I've missed a few calls," he said lamely.

"Hopefully, they'll get over it," she commented flippantly, and yawned as she stretched. At that moment, she glanced at his cell and couldn't help but notice that there was a string of messages from someone named Julia.

Julia? Who could have been calling Mike, repeatedly and perhaps frantically, at those late hours? She wondered if she had read Mike all wrong. Was he involved with someone? Was he a *player*? She had met too many men like that and had her fill of them. Images of a titled Englishman flashed in her mind—a man full of charm, beautifully coifed and dressed, whose sweet words flowed like the Thames. She had almost fallen for him when she realized the cad had three other women on the hook while he was sleeping with her. She threw Mike a cold-hearted glare. If he was like that, she would dump him like the morning trash.

Mike, listening quickly to just one of the voicemails, pursed his lips, feeling even more guilty. Missing dinner was bad enough, but not calling was inexcusable, and he knew it. He drew a deep breath and sighed before noticing that Jennifer was peering at him with a raised eyebrow. "Julia? Who's that?" The edge in her question signaled skepticism. Her expression left no doubt that Jennifer wondered whether the man who had made passionate love to her last night was a two-timing loser.

"I don't blame you for being confused, Jennifer," he said kindly. "Julia is my adult daughter—my only child. I promised Julia and her grandmother that I would be home for dinner and then—I forgot all about it. I didn't even call. I normally do that if there's a change in plans. Obviously they were worried," he confessed.

"Your daughter?" Jennifer responded. For some reason, Mike had never mentioned having a daughter. "And where is Julia's mother?"

A shadow crossed Mike's face. "She died," he related, looking sad.

"Oh, I'm sorry," Jennifer said softly. There was clearly a lot she did not yet know about this man.

"It's okay Jennifer," he said. "It was a long time ago. Julia was only five when she died, so it's been just the two of us. She worries when she doesn't know where I am."

"I understand Mike. I won't ask how your wife died..."

"You can ask. It was a car accident," he stated while caressing her arm. He liked Jennifer, but every time he thought of Phuong Ha his chest heaved and sadness flooded over him like a tidal wave. He managed a smile for Jennifer. "Last night was meaningful to me. I think it was to you as well."

Jennifer's words caught in her throat. She leaned over and kissed Mike on the forehead. "I apologize for my questioning you and for my doubting tone of voice, Mike. I looked over and saw several late night messages left by someone named Julia and thought the worst. Sorry. I know what a wonderful, honest man you are. It's just— well—we all have experiences that color our judgment and make us skeptical. I apologize for doubting you."

"In your place, I'd think the same thing," he stated.

"Maybe you should call her back, let her know you're okay, and apologize." Jennifer suggested.

"She's a big girl, and besides, she won't be up for another hour."

Jennifer cast her eyes to the clock. The gallery, located below her SoHo loft, wouldn't open for another hour and a half. "In that case," she said, lowering her voice and pulling Mike towards her, "I have a great idea on how we can kill an hour…" She kissed him with such desire he swore it made him forget his name. "I think I like this idea…" he whispered in her ear, obliging her command, and making love to her once again.

Afterwards, Jennifer went into her kitchen and came back with a breakfast tray. On it was a frothy cappuccino that she matched with a delicious croissant bursting with almond paste. Biting into it, Mike had to admit it melted in his mouth. Then he remembered Julia's anger and his mood darkened. He realized that dealing with Julia might not be so easy. His daughter had a worrisome streak of possessiveness. He really hoped that Jennifer and Julia would bond. Surely, Julia would be happy for him and welcome Jennifer. He hoped so.

By the time the gallery had opened its doors, Mike had returned to his office for a conference call with Michel Hepier & Co., his investment banking liaison in Paris that was working with him on a ship refinancing. Jennifer was back on the gallery floor, her face and neck still flushed a slight shade of red and her hair slightly tousled. As she walked around talking to prospective clients and young artists, Mike's warm kisses lingered in her thoughts exuding a fresh new sense of confidence and satisfaction. Her life had suddenly gotten a lot more interesting.

Chapter Nine

Jennifer sat in her office in front of her desktop Mac computer, staring blankly at the screen. Her thoughts kept going back to last night and she couldn't help daydreaming about Mike. She thought about the fact that he was a widower with a grown daughter. Mike's explanation had made her intensely curious. He'd explained that his late wife was a Vietnamese singer and actress named Phuong Ha. He mentioned an automobile accident he and Julia had survived, but didn't elaborate beyond that. Jennifer wanted to know more. She keyed his late wife's name into Google and found a rich ore of information in both Vietnamese and English.

She found it amazing that after eighteen years had elapsed since her death, there was still a Phuong Ha website honoring her memory. It contained multiple photos of her and videos of her singing. She did have a lovely voice, and was strikingly beautiful in a delicate porcelain-doll way. Jennifer wondered if Mike's daughter looked anything like her mother. Intriguingly, there were no photos of the daughter. She studied the site carefully, and conducted additional searches.

Phuong Ha had been a slender woman with long silky hair, a warm smile, and intelligent, dark eyes that drew people to her immediately. Her expression was theatrically hypnotizing and it was no wonder that she fascinated everyone.

Jennifer liked Mike. She liked him a lot. She had met a lot of interesting men, but too many of them had been so consumed with business and their careers that they had no clue as to how to talk to a woman. She found that most of them were conceited, self-centered, and boring. Mike was different. He talked about his daughter Julia in a way that made her seem like royalty. Clearly Julia was the princess, if not the queen, in his life. She hoped she could meet Julia soon, and that they would take to one another.

Jennifer admired Mike for more than his business acumen or his prowess in bed, and his concern for others. One day when they were walking along Fifth Avenue together, Mike had seen an elderly woman in distress. She was having trouble getting the attention of any cab drivers, so he had stopped to help and had gotten her into a cab.

Jennifer realized she could easily fall in love with this man. The thought was both exciting and scary. She had to know what kind of woman appealed to him. The fact that he had married this spectacular super-star seemed hardly surprising. Would she be able to step into PH's shoes and fulfill Mike as she had done? How could she possibly compete against PH's memory for his affections? She was definitely no superstar.

The website also contained biographical information about Mike. Apparently he had leveled with her about his own background as an American of French descent. She could imagine his ancestors as courageous, brawny, savvy heroes of the French-Indian war and America's own revolutionary war against King George III. He had good genes. The family history attested to that. He was a member of the Society of the Cincinnati, the nation's oldest patriotic organization, founded in 1783 by officers of the Continental Army and their French counterparts who served together in the American Revolution. Its membership included some of the country's most prestigious names.

Phuong Ha's biography intrigued her as well. She had been thirty-two at the time of the fatal car crash. She saw on the website that her family called her more familiarly by her initials— PH. PH had admired Audrey Hepburn and Princess Diana. That was understandable. She had the elegant look of Hepburn, in a little black Givenchy dress that transformed the fashion world, while Di exuded an eccentric mix of glamour and public service that had earned her the accolade, given to her by the then British Prime Minister Tony Blair, as "The People's Princess." Like Diana, PH had touched the hearts of millions of souls around the world for her selfless work in charitable activities.

Phuong Ha had also achieved a similar impact on so many through her music and her dedication to helping orphans. That had earned her respect, love and admiration across Vietnam. She could easily see why Mike had found her so attractive—not only for her outer beauty but her inner beauty as well. Charisma and character are notoriously difficult to define. Phuong Ha embodied the intangible qualities that defined both. Yet PH's love for Mike was not all that surprising.

Men like Mike were driven. They focused on objectives— then set out to realize them. Jennifer felt like she was tailored from the same cloth. Her family might have lacked the auspicious history of Mike's, but she had achieved success in her own right. She wasn't rich, but she did well, and her own hard work, sharp eye for artistic talent and keen negotiating skills had marked her as a rising art dealer.

She had lived in London for ten years. The art world there brimmed with activity and enabled her to make the kind of international connections through vigorous networking that proved pivotal to her ability to open a gallery in New York. At the time, she was living with her British beau, Hawkley Bronson, a graduate of Harrow and Oxford. Bronson had made his way at the Inner Temple as a successful barrister. But his conceit was wearing. He liked people but he loved himself more. His chauvinism translated into narcissism. He was proof that a British public school education was alive and well in the land of hope and glory. In hindsight, she regretted having a relationship with him.

Being seen on the arm of a polished Englishman who wore suits by Gieves & Hawkes and spoke in a posh upper class accent was fun, but she had realized that Hawkley viewed her as an ornament, not as a person. Life grew even more complicated when she also realized that the wives of Hawkley's friends viewed her as a threat. The last thing they would tolerate was someone with Jennifer's looks, intelligence, and charm winning the affections of their husbands. The wives would not put up with that. In their nuanced manner, they made clear to Jennifer that she was not welcome.

The last straw occurred after a particularly hard day of work at a St. James gallery. She had arrived home with groceries from Harrods's Market and deposited them in the kitchen, only to find Hawkley upstairs soaking in a hot bath and offering to do nothing for the dinner party due to commence later in the evening. She had climbed the stairwell of their lavish London flat, opened the bathroom door, and gazed down upon him fiercely as he sat in the tub, scrubbing his back with a long, silver-handled brush.

"Yes, darling?" He had purred. "Are we set for tonight? Table laid out? The Bollinger properly chilled? You know this crowd—it's tally-ho all the way!"

"Do you find the water to your liking?" she had asked sweetly, eyeing the bath and how well Hawkley was relaxing in the long tub.

"Perfection," he had cooed.

"I'm so glad," she had said. Then she took out a piece of paper on which she had written her goodbye note and casually handed it to him. "The lamb chops are in the ice box, daahhling," she sneered, "Make them your damn self. I'm out of here!" She blew him a farewell kiss, turned and left, leaving Hawkley speechless in the tub.

Within ten minutes she had packed her two suitcases, containing all her belongings and dragged them to the entrance on Hansen Place, where the black London taxi she had called for awaited her. She flew First Class to New York, and checked into the St. Regis Hotel. A week later she had leased the gallery space in SoHo and the loft above it to live in—and never looked back. It seemed so long ago...

Her thoughts drifted back to Mike. She had loved every minute of their recent time together. Glancing at the computer screen, she knew that Phuong Ha was hard to measure up to. While she was alive no woman could have competed with her for Mike's love. Jennifer hoped she could one day emulate PH's generous ways. She may not ever capture the hearts of many, but she hoped she would capture Mike's.

Chapter Ten

At Mike's country home, there was neither joy nor peace that morning. Julia had paced back and forth like a caged lioness in the kitchen, occasionally sipping her tea. Her father was still MIA. Van entered, wearing a light periwinkle blue embroidered Chanel robe. She saw that Julia was upset and walked over to give her distraught granddaughter a comforting hug before turning to pour herself a cup of tea as well. She waited for Julia to speak.

"Still no word from father," Julia said, unhappily.

"I am sure he was just working late last night," Van said, as she had the night before, still trying to reassure her. "Your father works late all the time."

"Yes, I know," Julia acknowledged, "but this time he didn't call, grandmother. He should have called. It would have taken just a few minutes." It was apparent from her furrowed brow and frustrated tone that she was worried and confused by her father's behavior. She resolved to insist that he tell her the truth about why he didn't come home, where he was, and why he didn't call. The rest of the world could hide its face from her behind a façade, but she expected her father to come clean.

"Julia, I'm sure your father is fine and will be home for dinner tonight," Van said. "Now, finish your tea. The car is waiting for you outside. You need to get to your acting class before you're late." Julia sighed, hugged her grandmother goodbye, and left for school.

****

Towards evening Van padded through the elegant living room dressed in an intricately hand-embroidered purple dress created by her favorite designer in Ho Chi Minh City. She sat at the polished Steinway grand piano and played the first movement, marked *allegro*, of Mozart's *Sonata No. 16*, known as the *Sonata semplice*. It was a short sonata, only fourteen minutes in duration, yet, as with most of the master's work, the notes were elegant and memorable. Mozart had written down the composition during a visit to Munich for the production of *La finta giardiniera* in 1774. The music echoed across the Scandinavian mahogany furniture and stark white walls lined by the post-impressionist art of Henri Martin and Edouard Vuillard.

She usually reserved this hobby for evenings, and tonight she especially felt the need for soothing tones. Van loved music, especially Phuong Ha's music, from her traditional folk songs to her modern compositions. Overall, Van's tastes were classical. Frederic Chopin's three piano sonatas challenged her. Even great pianists found them difficult to play. Celebrated for his piano miniatures, his romanticism was known for its feeling. Haydn ranked as the final member of her trio favorite composers. She especially loved his piano sonata in E-flat major and would play it often

Julia entered, wearing a black dress. Black frequently characterized her attire when she attended acting class. She glanced around the room. Besides the awesome collection of modern art, one whole wall had been set aside for photographs of her mother. Some depicted her in performance. Some showed her hugging a smiling Julia. Others featured Mike, Julia, and Van. A few captured Van with other family members still in Vietnam. Looking at these photographs revived Van's warm memories of family. They were graphic depictions of the poetry of a loving family life. Julia identified with them as well.

The ones that touched her most immediately were those of her with Mike.

There was a whole row of these. Photos captured them together at London Bridge, the Eiffel Tower, the Brandenburg Gate, dining at Le Quatro in Rome, purchasing a luxurious handbag for Van in Florence, and riding a camel in Egypt beside the Great Pyramid. There were even photographs of her accompanying her father to events with his business associates—photographs in which Julia splendidly filled the role that her mother would have played. Her mother would have been proud, she knew.

"I see you are wearing black again," Van commented.

"Yes, grandmother. It's a New York thing."

People in New York loved black, wearing it as a badge of gravitas. For Julia, wearing black made her feel as if she was fitting in. *When in Rome, do as the Romans do.* New York was no different. You looked like New Yorkers and acted like them, or they discounted you. Her language problems created enough of a barrier and her Asian background complicated that issue. So if all the women in the class wore black, she had resolved that she would, too. She would accord her classmates no additional reasons to look down on her.

Today had been tough. Igor had insisted that the class do a scene from Alan Jay Lerner and Frederic Lowe's hit Broadway musical, *My Fair Lady.* The play centers on the efforts of phonetics expert Henry Higgins to teach ill-educated women to speak like aristocrats. He shares that obsession with his chum Colonel Pickering. Convinced that he can teach a lowly flower girl to speak proper English, he latches onto Eliza Doolittle as the subject for his transformation. The play was based on Bernard Shaw's *Pygmalion*, which unlike the musical has a hard edge and ends unhappily. Igor had advised the class that the book had more wit then the play, and was perfect for practicing elocution of the Queen's English.

The challenge of speaking in an English accent had thrilled most of the class, even though none of them proved especially adept at it. For them the exercise was a joke. Igor had enjoyed teaching the students to enunciate their vowels more to the front of their tongue and to get away from the American habit of speaking from the throat. Teaching Shaw made Igor feel like *he* was Henry Higgins. He played the role to the hilt, even assuming the mannerisms of an English professor.

Julia had been doing well in class until now. This challenging exercise had proven a humiliating nightmare. She had enough trouble normally in enunciating the American version of English and its informal colloquialisms. A formal English accent presented a hopeless venture.

Julia fumbled through her lines, "Lovely day for a bit of a stroll, Governor."

"Not good enough, Julia, you sounded like a squawking chicken! Try again! You must BECOME the character!" Igor passionately scolded.

"Lovely day for a bit of a stroll, Gov'na." Julia said again: this time with a better accent.

She had struggled with every word. By contrast, her classmates seemed to sail through the assignment. They had done better than she had and they were quick to let her know it.

"Can't get the accent?" Vicky had said sweetly, as if trying to help.

"Hard," Julia had said, saying as little as possible.

"Takes the right talent," Vicky had said airily.

"Just practice," Julia countered

Linda had joined them. She looked Julia straight in the eye. "Can I ask a question?"

Julia hesitantly nodded with suspicion.

"Why are you even in this class if you can't speak English properly?"

Jason stopped the sniping before things got too ugly. He jumped in between the two angry women and pointedly addressed Linda to her face. "Hey, Linda, is it true that your uncle might be indicted on corruption charges?" he asked. He spoke like a man wielding a sharp dagger. "I read about it in the *New York Post*. Man, he looks *baaad*."

Linda, whose manner might have been designed to make people believe she was descended from the Queen of England, shriveled. She tightened her lips, shot him a nasty look, turned on her heels and stormed off, much to Julia's delight. Julia flashed Jason a smile. He lightly brushed his hand against hers. She felt a jolt, a delightful jolt, and smiled.

Vicky stood nearby absorbing this exchange, and glared at Jason. "She was just trying to help," she snottily advised.

Jason placed his hand across his heart. "You are so full of it, babe," he said caustically. Vicky would have loved for Jason to address her as *babe* had he shown any romantic interest in her but it was obvious he was putting her down. She gave him an evil look and walked over to where Linda was standing.

"They are just not nice people," Jason said to Julia.

Julia nodded. "Not nice at all."

"Main thing, kiddo: do not let them live inside your head. Every minute you do is one minute more than they deserve to be there. You're better than they are and they know it. They're just jealous."

"They will never accept me, Jason," she said sadly.

"As classmates and competitors, no," he agreed. "All because they envy you. But there's a life beyond this acting class." He smiled down at her. "You amaze me. Everything about you is neat." He glanced at Linda, whose antics made her seem shrill, not funny, as she acted out in front of the other girls. "They're not worth one inch of you," he said, turning to leave.

Julia appreciated Jason's encouragement. Still, while Jason uplifted her spirits, she fought to suppress her insecurity. She looked at Vicky and Linda. These fellow students had been mean as they mocked her attempts at both a Cockney and upper-class English accent. Weary of their nonsense, Igor had literally slapped them on the wrist after botching a scene. Banging a ruler against a chair, he termed the efforts of the two spoiled brats, "Unremarkable and nothing to feel superior about," he said.

The two girls had taken it out on Julia, behind her back making fun of Julia's inability to get her lines right. In the play, speaking the word "loverly" in bad English is funny or charming, depending upon one's view of flower girls at the turn of the century. Julia had managed to mangle the word, setting off their laughter.

Igor picked up on their antics. Infuriated, he chastised the entire class. "Oh, and you all are so perfect, the rest of you?! Shame on you all!" he scolded. No less angry, Jason had stood up and backed up Igor's harsh words about jealousy and unprofessionalism. Igor then worked diligently with Julia to help her speak the lines correctly. She appreciated the gesture. Still, she wondered if Igor's Henry Higgins act was just that— an act, not the action of a sensitive teacher committed to reassuring a reluctant student.

The exercise had proven a debacle for everyone. Clearly Igor was more at home with Chekov and Shakespeare than with English drawing room comedy. He had compensated for his deficiency by taking on the airs of the very people whom Shaw, and then Lerner & Lowe, had made fun of. He became a caricature of himself. For the moment, she felt sorry for Igor. He was a good guy, but flawed. *Well, who isn't*, she thought.

Julia had been smart enough to see that Igor had his insecurities and pretensions too. Her bumbling classmates thought he was a genius. Even as they made fun of her, their dumb behavior caused her to ask herself if acting was right for her. In truth, failure was not an option. She had been stoic on the outside. After the final run-through of *My Fair Lady,* when Linda and Vicky blew their lines, Julia had calmly stared them down and used her bad English to mock their names. She began to deliberately refer to Vicky as Boomsy and Linda as Ti Ti. She did it in front of other students. It was a defining moment.

Julia's gambit had struck a responsive chord. Her classmates turned their scorn on the two girls, using those names as well. Jason, always supportive, had given Julia the high-sign and laughed at how deftly Julia had deliberately mangled their names and cut them down a notch. The victory might have been small, but it gave Julia a new sense of pride.

By the last few classes, she was getting the hang of things. In the final session, she addressed the Henry Higgins character perfectly. She called him, "my dear man" with the finesse of a Royal Shakespeare Company leading lady. Such excellence marked a significant step forward. Yet Julia worried that no matter how hard she strived, enunciating English correctly might prove a bridge too far. In her heart Julia knew she was smart. Surely putting her mind to it she would succeed!

Returning home after class, Julia entered the living room to the sound of Van's beautiful piano playing. Seeing her granddaughter's discouraged expression Van took her hands off the piano and looked at Julia, then said gently, "Julia, why so unhappy?"

Julia described how she had struggled with the accents and Vicky and Linda's mockery. "They were vicious, grandma," she said. "Why do people have to be like that?"

Van regarded Julia with a wan smile. "The world is like that. Not everyone is nice. Do not trouble yourself with them. Trust me, they will get their due. You just must continue to do your best, and don't worry about what such people think of you. "Van got up from the piano bench to give Julia a hug. "You are much loved, Julia."

Julia returned the hug. "Has papa come home?"

Van looked at her with thoughtful eyes. "Your father will be home soon, I am sure.

Van had a way of erasing Julia's frowns. "Really sure?"

Her grandmother nodded.

Julia returned her grandmother's look. "I still can't believe papa never came home last night. Why isn't he here now?" Van declined to take the bait. She felt that whatever Mike did, Julia would always occupy the front row seat in his life. She changed the subject. "I'm pleased to hear that you are mastering this play. It is an American classic. You, child, will be an American classic."

Julia gave her a wan look. "Are you certain, grandma?"

"I'm certain," Van said. She refused to tolerate Julia's self-indulgence when she sounded sorry for herself.

"Papa makes me angry," Julia said.

Van was suddenly quite alarmed. "Why?" Van asked softly, trying to feel her granddaughter out. She wondered: what exactly was going on here. Why this intense possessiveness?

"I need him to be here and he's not," Julia said, sounding like a child. She added, "I need to talk to him." She ignored the comfort-

94

ing hand Van offered. "Papa is leaving me alone. He promised he would never do that." She gazed fiercely upon her grandmother. "*He promised.*" For a moment she was back on the steps of the library in Shanghai, where one day she had waited over an hour, alone and frightened, till he arrived to pick her up, late and very apologetic. He hoisted his trembling daughter in his arms, hugged her, and promised never, ever to leave her alone and frightened again. He never had until now.

Chapter Eleven

Mike arrived home later that evening for dinner with a smile on his face and a sense that fate had renewed his life. His coat and tie were neatly in place. It occurred to Van that Mike looked remarkably fresh for someone whose excuse for missing egg rolls the night before was working late and falling asleep on his office coach. Meantime Mike had breezed into the living room and was placing a quick kiss on her cheek. Van's face lit up and she accepted Mike's enthusiastic greeting. He did seem chipper.

"Where's Julia?" he asked, looking around sheepishly.

"In the library, Mike. Studying."

"That's my girl," he said. Being away from her for a day made him long to see her.

Van's face turned somber. "Mike, you disappointed Julia last night. She had a really bad time. You left her confused. She worried why you didn't come home last night or call. I tried to reassure her that you were fine. But she was terrified that something had happened."

Mike understood but felt resentful. He was a grown man. No one, not even his daughter, had the right to subject him to a curfew.

"Van, look, I'm sorry if I upset Julia, but she's not a child," he said. Then he lied. "We're wrestling with a huge deal. You know how these things go. Everybody wants to change everything at the last minute. I'm getting to where my distaste for lawyers has changed to outright hatred."

Van nodded, persuaded. Mike was entitled to the benefit of the doubt. "Well, you are right. You don't need to answer to anyone. Still, your habit has been to check in with Julia when you're late or your plans change. Your daughter expects an explanation. She deserves one."

Van gave his appearance close scrutiny. Noticing her assessment of his clothing he responded, "You mean why don't I look half dead? It's called the New York Athletic Club. A hot shower and keeping a spare new shirt on hand brings you back from the dead."

"Good. But don't tell me. Tell Julia."

Mike entered the library, where Julia was seated at the desk, clearly studying some lines. She looked up.

She lit into him. "Where *were* you, papa?" Julia demanded, tears in her eyes, her English half-garbled, as happened when she was upset. "Why you not call, or answer me? Why you not home for egg rolls last night? Grandma very upset. We work hard all day! Special egg rolls just for you!"

Mike pursed his lips. Missing dinner was bad enough. That he hadn't called was inexcusable. "I'm sorry, Julia," he stammered. "I was working late last night and, well, I got hung up. I should have called. I thought about the egg rolls, later, before I finally got to bed, how wonderful I knew they would be and how you and Van worked so hard to prepare them just for me. It was just way too late to return your calls. I can't stand it that I upset you, Princess. Forgive me?"

He had messed up. Yet as deeply as he loved Julia, he realized that the time had come to begin living his own life again. No one could replace PH. That did not mean he had spent the rest of his days alone. Julia filled an enormous gap in his life. But she was his daughter. If a new love came into his life, wasn't he entitled to that happiness? He started to tell Julia about Jennifer, then thought better of it. The time clearly was not right. Confession would infuriate Julia.

He tried soothing her, "Let's have a nice, pleasant family dinner, okay?" he begged. I can't wait to eat the egg rolls if you have any left." He pulled her to her feet and wrapped his arms around her. "Don't be angry Princess," he begged.

"All right, papa," Julia said, with a resigned sigh.

Seated at the dining room table, Mike smiled at Julia and Van while he raved over the reheated egg rolls, devouring them with a gigantic appetite. Between bites he asked Julia what was new in her acting class. Surprisingly, Van answered, in a jocular tone: "I think our Julia has a boyfriend."

"What?" Mike asked, surprised. "You're kidding. Who is he?"

Van shook her head. "One of her classmates." Julia rolled her eyes at her Grandmother.

"American?"

"What is the phase you use— ah, yes—*true blue*."

"Have you met him?"

Van shook her head. "No, but maybe soon. I think she has invited him to our apartment to work on a play together."

Mike was grinning, hope etched into his face. "Great. Let him come over so we can meet him. The sooner, the better."

"Grandma, stop. Papa, I do not have a boyfriend. He's just a classmate. A friend. He said he would help me with my English. I don't want to talk about Jason. That's his name, since you are so curious."

Mike's eyes twinkled as an idea popped into his mind. "Look, I want to meet this Jason friend."

Julia sighed. "There's no need, Papa. He's just a friend. Though a good friend and a nice guy."

"All the more reason to meet him," Mike maintained. He looked at Van then turned back to Julia. "All right, I have an idea. I think we've all spent too much time by ourselves." His eyes roved the room. "You know what I think we could use, at our house in West-chester?"

"What?" Julia asked.

"A party," he pronounced. "That big house—and us—what's needed there is a party." He pointed a friendly finger at Julia. "I sure hope you're inviting Jason."

"What if you don't like him?" Julia asked. "You're a snob, you know."

Mike reared his head. "I am not!" He exclaimed. Julia's charge threw him slightly off balance. "Look, why don't you invite your entire acting class—and your teacher. Hopefully they will all want to see each other socially, and this party would give them that chance."

"Maybe—but what kind of party?" she asked.

"What kind of party would you like?" he responded.

Julia thought for a moment. She gave Van a playful look, and, the gleam back in her eye, turned to Mike. "A costume party! I think that would make it more fun!"

Mike pretended to meditate on the suggestion, then assented. "Why not? Great idea." Turning to Van, he said, "We can order the food from E.A.T. on Madison Avenue. They make your favorite cakes. We can have it delivered up here."

Julia took her time to respond. "Thank you, papa. I have another idea: Since that house is best for a large crowd, can we send a mini-bus to take the city people there and back? That would be a nice way to get everyone from my acting class to say yes."

Mike held out his hand and Julia shook it. "Done!" Mike exclaimed.

"I do love you, papa," Julia said.

He lifted her hand and kissed it. "I know, Princess. I love you too."

Van beamed. Once again all was well in their little world.

Chapter Twelve

The Roaring Twenties, also known as the Jazz Age, was a happy time, supported by a sense of optimism and a belief that the future would be prosperous. Wild costumes and fringed dresses defined fashion for the era. It was the decade of bathtub gin and people zipping around in the newest cutting edge Model T automobiles. The party that Julia designed aimed to capture the exuberance and high spirits of the Jazz Age.

Given that the invitation Julia sent out was about capturing the glamour of a bygone era, most of the female guests showed up in roaring twenties fashion. The women wore short flapper-style dresses adorned with a beaded fringe. Their hair was pinned up in a fashionable "bobbed" style of the decade, capped off with feather headbands. The men were dressed to the nines as well in high-waisted three-piece zoot suits and bowler hats. The costumes many of the guests wore that evening bore 1920s names like "Nile Green," "Sunset Orange," and "French Blue."

Always one to break with tradition and stand out from the crowd, Julia appeared in a black dress with pearls and a tiara, which was more of a 1950s fashion statement. She looked eerily like an Asian Audrey Hepburn's character Holly Golightly in the movie *Breakfast at Tiffany's*. The character was revered for her charisma, and the film had become legendary. Hubert de Givenchy had designed the black dress Hepburn wore in the film. It had proved to be more than iconic. It shifted cultural tastes in fashion for women from the staid look of the 1950s to a sleek, modern sensibility.

Tonight Julia recreated Hepburn's beauty and charm. Her lithe, slender figure fit the look of Hepburn perfectly. The long black cigarette holder she held completed the look, achieving fashion perfection. Julia stood out as the most glamorous person at the party. She had brushed off Mike and Van's compliments beforehand as expected flattery, but had swelled with pride as guests echoed their sentiment.

A secret side of her suggested that she had the potential, in theatre and perhaps film, to establish herself as the next Hepburn. *Wouldn't that be something*, she told herself as she admired her reflection one last time in the dressing room's full-length mirror. She knew that her mother had aspired to be a movie star. Like Julia, she too had admired Hepburn. In looking to Hepburn, Julia was channeling her mother. Phuong Ha had tragically not lived to fulfill that role. Julia was determined to complete what she felt her mother had commenced.

As the party began, Julia was full of excitement and good cheer, hugging and welcoming the guests. Jason Rodriguez, her admirer and theatre classmate, arrived in a red leather jacket and sporting the stubble on his face that had become the fashion statement for millennial men. In Mike's view, these young males all looked like they needed a shower and a shave, but he realized there wasn't much to be gained worrying about a passing trend. He had to admit that even with the stubble, Julia's friend Jason was a handsome and pleasant-looking young man.

Dressed in a dark suit, bright tie, and top hat, Mike was the picture of 1920s elegance. Van was too. Tonight she was wearing a long floral flapper dress with a matching 1920s cloche hat. Her warm, gracious presence set a welcoming tone for the festivities.

The food was glorious. E.A.T. had outdone itself with cream cakes and strawberries, fresh salmon, Brie de Melun, Bleu D'auvergne, and Beaufort cheese. The food company had, as always, flown in fresh delicacies from Paris, along with a succulent variety of hors d'oeuvres. The wine was top notch and the liquor top shelf, of course. A small jazz band served up a medley of tunes from the jazz era, like 'Ain't Been Misbehavin,' that beckoned people to dance the Foxtrot and Peabody, which were popular at the time.

Van pulled Mike to the side, proud that the idea of the party was going so well. She pointed to Julia and Jason on the dance floor, doing the Charleston.

"This is exactly what Julia needed," she commented, cheerful mirth in her eyes. She looked at the fifty or so guests, laughing and talking. "I am glad your friends and staff came. So did Julia's entire class—and her teacher. Julia has wonderful friends. She needs to know that they like her. I don't think she sees that. If they didn't like her they would not have come here, all dressed in their costumes, to share this evening with her."

Mike threw the crowd a passing glance. He was feeling pleased with his idea of throwing a party. He was convinced that the worst thing for Julia was her tendency to feel isolated, a bi-racial Asian-American trapped between two cultures. He looked at Julia fondly as she and Jason flirted. "Jason's a nice kid, Van," Mike said.

Van nodded approvingly. "He's well-mannered. That counts for a lot," she agreed.

"Well, there's always hope, isn't there?" Mike joked. "As long as he makes Julia happy then I'm happy," he said.

Jason broke away from Julia and approached them. He bowed his head respectfully towards Van and smiled at Mike. "Great party," he uttered. "I mean, this is terrific. Thank you so much for inviting me—for inviting all of us in the class." He lowered his voice. "Personally I think this is great for Julia."

Mike smiled brightly. "We were just saying the same thing. Enjoy the party, Jason. You're always welcome in our home."

"Thank you, Sir," Jason said.

"Yes, feel welcome here," Van added.

Mike beamed as he moved around the room, chatting with various guests. A little while later he noticed that Igor, Julia's acting coach, had arrived and was chatting with Van. Igor was dressed stylishly in a black suit with a scarlet shirt and a white silk cravat. He had a broad smile that displayed a row of perfect white teeth. Naturally self-confident, Igor took note of the guests and was pleased to see his entire class there as well as the types of people Julia's father had clearly invited. Igor was a bit of an elitist. He had accepted the invitation out of a sense of obligation, but seeing the obviously affluent crowd of Mike Chamonix's other guests, he was thrilled to be there.

After giving Julia a hug, he chatted with Van, then intercepted a waiter carrying a silver tray and took a glass of Bollinger champagne. He lifted his glass, locked eyes with Julia across the room, and raised his glass in a toast. She smiled and returned his toast by waving her cigarette holder.

Julia smiled as she turned back to Jason. The smile turned into a scowl as she saw Vicky heading straight towards them. Against Julia's initial instinct, Mike had persuaded her to invite that particular classmate as a gesture of friendship—despite Vicky and Linda's demeaning behavior. There was cold irony in Vicky's appearance. While other guests had dressed in 1920s attire, Vicky was the only one besides Julia who wore a 1950s era costume. She had come dressed as Marilyn Monroe. Interestingly, it was Marilyn Monroe, not Audrey Hepburn, who had been the first choice for the role of Holly Golightly. With her platinum blonde hair, curvy hips and bright red lipstick, Vicky could have passed as the legendary movie star's double.

Vicky was mean-spirited, but when she wanted something, she could turn on the charm. She gave Jason a searching glance that seemed to invite possibilities. There was a flush on his face as she chatted with him. He felt uncomfortable. Julia had deliberately walked away, and he kept looking around the room for her. Jason had one interest, and one only—and he didn't want Julia to misinterpret his being polite to a classmate as anything else.

Stone-faced, Julia watched this little scene unfold. She might have obsessed further, except that her attention was diverted. The downstairs front doorbell rang, and a housekeeper opened the door. From the second-floor balcony that overlooked the entrance Julia could see that a strange woman had arrived. As Jennifer entered, Mike went up to her immediately and they kissed. Julia froze, shocked. *Who was this woman? Why was her father kissing her?* Her lips tightened. *Why had he not told her he was seeing someone?* She stormed over to Van.

"Who is that woman?" she asked Van, turning her head towards Mike and Jennifer as they came up the staircase to the main room. Mike's arm was wrapped protectively around Jennifer's slim waist. Watching them enter the crowd, Julia's eyes blazed.

"I don't know who she is, Julia. Obviously a friend," Van said, curtly.

"Did you know about this?" Julia shot back.

"No, child, I did not. But listen..." She lowered her voice and softened her tone. "I am not altogether surprised that something like this might be happening." She gave a wistful smile. "Julia, we cannot expect your father, a handsome, successful man in the prime of his life, to remain alone forever."

"He is not alone," Julia breathed. He has—us. "She ran a critical eye over Jennifer as Mike introduced her to people. They held hands as they made the rounds, enraging Julia.

Just then Igor came over to speak with Van again. Julia broke away to talk to Bethany, the one classmate she felt close to besides Jason.

Van was asking Igor a question: "Igor, have you thought to give the class one of the Shakespearean plays to do as their graduation project? I know you teach your students to read him. You could go a step further, and provide them an opportunity to put their scholarship onto the stage. Just an old lady's suggestion, so forgive me if I am out of line."

Igor reflected somberly. "That is an excellent idea. I will think about it, but perhaps not for graduation. I am not sure the class is ready to do such profound plays."

"Yes, I can see what you mean," Van said politely, impressed by Igor's manner more than his sweeping generalization. She glanced at Julia, and pressed her argument. "But, as you may know, Julia studies Shakespeare hard. She is a fine scholar. You must give her every opportunity to prove herself."

"You know I will," Igor promised. "Julia is one of my best students. She has a tremendous future ahead of her."

Igor's praise meant a lot to Julia, who overheard his last statement from where she was standing, just a few feet away. At the same time, she couldn't keep her eyes off her father and Jennifer. She also noted that Jason remained in deep conversation with Vicky. In fairness, Vicky seemed to be doing most of the talking, Julia acknowledged. She was certainly working hard to keep Jason in conversation with her.

Julia didn't blame Jason. Vicky at her best could command the attention of any male. She was pretty and had a nice shape. Looking at her body language with Jason, as she moved in even closer, Julia felt certain that Vicky knew how to use that body to manipulate men. She wasn't jealous. She knew she was more interesting. In any event, Jason was not her boyfriend, and he had every right to flirt with other girls.

Julia knew she could best Vicky. But the intimate looks Jennifer and Mike were exchanging were a different matter. It struck her that they seemed too well acquainted to qualify as business associates. There was something possessive in Jennifer's manner as she hooked her arm through Mike's.

She observed Mike whisper in Jennifer's ear, prompting Jennifer to laugh happily. Jennifer was well put together. She was wearing a smart, avant-garde one-shoulder beige bandage dress that wound tightly around her boyish hips and small bosom. Her confident body language and alluring smile commanded Mike's attention. Julia had a sudden premonition that a shark-in-disguise had arrived. The problem with sharks, she thought, was that while they might be hypnotic, their bite could be fatal.

Chapter Thirteen

"Julia, meet Jennifer," Mike said, hope filling his face. He gave Jennifer's hand a friendly squeeze. She looked at him sweetly, then gave Julia a warm smile, thrilled to be meeting her new boyfriend's daughter.

"Hi Julia," she beamed. "Your father has told me all about you. I gather we'll be seeing you on Broadway, and then the silver screen." Jennifer's tone was vibrant but her words—her praise—were not well-received. *Her father had been talking to this woman about her?*

Julia knew she had to be civil. She ran her eyes over Jennifer, hoping for a more complete assessment of the woman. She perceived a rival. Jennifer in turn recognized that winning over Mike's only child was going to present hurdles. Well, she thought, *it is what it is. I may be standing in the cross-hairs now, but in time I will win over this young woman.*

Julia noticed that Jennifer's hair was bundled around her head in a French twist, a hair style that suggested formality and business. For a party like this, she would have expected the woman's ash-blonde hair to flow gently around her shoulders. And while she was wearing what was clearly a designer outfit, this particular dress seemed tight, deliberately worn tonight to show off her slender, well-toned body.

Instantly disliking Jennifer, the one thing crossing Julia's mind was how to rid her father of this scourge. Keeping a tight smile required all she could muster.

"Hello. Nice to meet you Jennifer," she managed in an even tone. "Tell me. How do you know my papa?"

Her *papa*. How odd, Jennifer thought. Julia sounded like a five-year-old. She forced a smile. "Your father is a collector of fine art. I'm a dealer. I buy and sell internationally. Your father wanted a Marc Chagall. I think it might even be a present for a certain daughter."

"Jennifer," Mike said with feigned annoyance. "You're spoiling the surprise."

"Well," Jennifer proclaimed, "your father has excellent taste. This is a special Chagall."

Julia looked at Mike. "You said you were going to, remember? So you already bought it for me, papa? Really?"

"Really," Mike nodded. He drew himself up. "Just for you, darling. As I promised."

"Thank you," Julia said happily. Whatever her feelings about Jennifer, it excited her that her father had taken pains to acquire a significant piece of art he believed would make his daughter happy.

"We also got a Warhol," Jennifer added.

"Andy Warhol?"

"One and the same," Jennifer said. "I've found a screen he did of Mick Jagger. It's an extraordinary process. The screens he did were originally made of silk. Then he shifted to nylon and polyester because they last longer and provide a sharper print."

"It sounds complicated," Julia said.

"Very. Warhol was adept at using different colors to achieve a layering effect. The same original image produced different color compositions," Jennifer added.

"It's for my office," Mike said effusively. "I've always wanted one of the ones he did of Jagger."

"Doesn't Mick Jagger own them?" Julia wondered.

Jennifer interjected, "You are absolutely right, Julia. Mick Jagger has a few. But Warhol did multiple versions of each silk screen."

Jennifer was happy to show off her expertise.

Julia eyed her father. "So the Warhol will make your office look nicer?"

"You bet!" her father enthused.

"Julia," Jennifer said, "I look forward to our getting to know one another. Mike has told me how special you are."

Julia nodded curtly, the smile growing smaller.

Well, this didn't seem to be going too badly, Mike thought. He smiled at Julia hopefully. "Okay, great. Glad you guys met. We'll see you later, Princess. Great party, don't you think?" Without waiting for a response, he took Jennifer by the elbow and steered her over to meet Van. Julia decided to follow, staying a few paces behind.

Van greeted Jennifer warmly. "If Mike likes you I am impressed. He is picky, you know."

Jennifer laughed. "Oh, boy—do I know!" She touched Mike on the arm. "He's been after me for weeks to meet you and Julia. I'm terribly happy to have the opportunity." She cast an approving eye over the house. "I love your home. It's so sleek. I love the way the outside light just floods the interior. And your views of the country-side are breathtaking."

"Thank you," Van replied, flattered. "We like it. It expresses our joyful spirit."

"Well, it has an uplifting ethos. You feel it the minute you walk through the front door."

"Thank you," Van said, appreciating Jennifer's enthusiasm. Noticing Julia lurking behind Mike, she addressed her granddaughter. "The house has a spirit of its own. Don't you agree, Julia?"

"Oh yes, It's a wonderful house," Julia said without enthusiasm.

"Mike picked out the architect and he and Julia both worked with him to make it perfect," Van added.

Julia's expression remained cold and disinterested. She crossed her arms as Van, Jennifer, and Mike chatted.

Sensing Jennifer's unease, Mike said. "Hey, how about a personalized tour of the place? Just no taking any of our art. Not for sale."

"I would hope not," Jennifer laughed. She stepped away and her eye focused on the grouping of signed Picasso lithographs that lined one wall. The one that caught her eye was a 1901 hand-signed piece of a husband and wife kissing in the bedroom. The white sheets on the bed counterpointed the turquoise blue walls. The scene was tender and intimate, and defined why Picasso's work was remarkable.

"Julia, would you like to accompany us?" Mike asked.

"You and Jennifer go ahead," Julia said sourly. She made no effort to conceal her coolness to Jennifer. Mike and Jennifer chose to ignore her dismissive demeanor.

"Sure?" Jennifer asked, reaching out to Julia.

"I will look after our other guests."

"Okay, then," Mike said. "Don't say we didn't offer."

As Mike and Jennifer walked off, Julia watched her father put his arm around Jennifer's slender waist and steer her around, pausing in front of each painting in order to explain how it had been acquired.

Van gave Julia a look. What was wrong with her? She had never acted this strangely. Her normal warmth had turned to ice. Of course Mike had never brought a woman home before. Julia's dark eyes glowered as Van walked over to her.

"Julia, you were being rude. Jennifer was nice to you."

"She would be nice to anyone she thought could benefit her," Julia said tartly.

"Julia, stop it. You don't know this woman. We all just met," Van rejoined.

Julia persisted. She pointed a slender finger at Jennifer as she walked down the hallway with Mike. "Look at her. See how she is hanging on papa's every word?"

"Don't we all? Besides, she obviously likes him."

"She likes the fact that we have money, grandmother. It's obvious that she's a gold-digger. I'm not going to let her take advantage of my father."

"Julia!" Van scolded, shocked at her granddaughter's immediate fierce dislike of a woman Mike clearly had feelings for. Van felt it was an encouraging sign. He had loved PH dearly, but after almost twenty years Van was happy to see him move to the next stage of his life. Julia's behavior appalled her. Why was she trying to erect a barrier between Mike and his new romantic interest?

Mike was also confused and disappointed. He loved his daughter and did not want to see her hurt. But she would have to accept the situation.

Van hoped that Julia would come around. She knew Mike's daughter had no choice. "Get to know someone before you judge, Julia," she advised.

"I'm right. I know I am right," Julia said defiantly.

"Your hostility is unwarranted," Van said.

"You wait and see," she forecast.

Julia returned to her other guests. Vicky had moved on from Jason and was busy making herself the life of the party, flirting with two other young men from their theater class. Meantime Jason was engaged in a heavy conversation with Igor. Julia threw one more wicked glance at Jennifer as she and Mike disappeared around a corner. Then she joined Jason.

"Hey there," Jason said, looking down at the lovely young woman on whom he had a mad crush. He was feeling a little overwhelmed. His middle class background was modest compared to this kind of wealth. Julia was the object of his affection but way out of his humble reach. She lived in a penthouse in the city and now he discovered her family also had this incredible mansion.

"Hey yourself," Julia responded, smiling warmly up at him. Jason's admiration always made her feel good. It was good that her father knew this popular and handsome American man really liked his daughter. Maybe it would make him jealous.

"Ah, my two finest students!" Igor interjected, coming between them and putting an arm around each of their shoulders, in a brief show of affection.

"You mean that?" Julia asked.

"Do I mean it?" Igor said in an incredulous voice, relishing the moment. "How could any objective teacher conclude otherwise?"

Jason clasped Julia's arm. "I trust you will give Julia the chance to become a star?"

"She was born one," Igor commented. He looked closely at her outfit. "You are an *incarnation* of the late Audrey Hepburn. Even she would have to agree. Don't you think so, Jason?"

Jason stared at Julia. The sun was shining in through the floor-to-ceiling picture windows, casting a magical light on her. To his lovesick eyes she had never looked lovelier. "Amen," he intoned, his voice cracking a little.

Feeling both pairs of eyes on her, Julia reveled in the admiration.

Then her father returned and her mood darkened. Why was he holding hands with that terrible woman? *Why couldn't she just go away? Better yet why couldn't she just die?* Mike was hers, and only hers, and she wasn't about to share him with this heinous viper.

Chapter Fourteen

Julia and Mike sat in their front row orchestra seats, clapping as the final curtain lowered on *Miss Saigon*, currently in yet another revival at the Broadway Theatre between West 52nd and West 53rd Streets.

The musical, written by Claude-Michel Schönberg and Alain Boublil, with lyrics by Boublil and Richard Maltby, Jr., had premièred at the Theatre Royal, Drury Lane, London, on September 20, 1989, then opened on Broadway at the Broadway Theatre on April 11, 1991. Kim was played by Lea Salonga, a Filipino actress and singer, first in the West End in London in '89 and then on Broadway in '91. There are two revivals. Eva Maria Noblezada, of Filipino-American descent, portrayed Kim both, in London and New York.

Mike had chosen *Miss Saigon* because he knew that Igor was talking about using the play as one of the vehicles for giving Julia a perfect opportunity to show the full extent of her craft in class. Mike felt that seeing the play performed by a top-tier Broadway cast would give Julia ideas on how to portray a complicated lead character. This might even be a role she could take on herself someday, on the world stage.

He believed that Julia could benefit from watching it on other levels too, sensing that his daughter was experiencing her own identity crisis. Seeing her frustration was painful. He loved his daughter and knew that she deserved far better than the cruel teasing and back-biting that characterized the mean-spirited behavior of at least a few of Julia's classmates.

Mike had tremendous faith in Julia. He knew how incredibly talented she was. He felt confident that, while struggles lay on the path ahead, she would rise above them. He was resolved to do everything possible to help her see that, not just despite her Asian background, but largely *because* of it, her talent would in time allow her to securely cross over into the fluid dynamic that characterized American culture.

To his surprise, Julia had a very different reaction to the play than he expected. She initially seemed delighted that he was taking her to see a revival of *Miss Saigon*. She was familiar with the story and knew it was a Broadway echo of Puccini's classic opera, *Madame Butterfly*, a tragedy of broken love, cultural identity and a mother's tragic sacrifice. The opera embodied the attitudes of 19th century American imperialism that prevailed at the time. Mike hoped that seeing *Miss Saigon* would lift Julia's spirits if she imagined herself in the title role. Instead it had deeply depressed her, and solidified her concerns.

Mike believed that Americans welcomed foreigners into their midst if they were willing to integrate themselves into American culture. However, this musical conveyed the opposite conclusion. Obviously what was being portrayed in this story were attitudes that no longer existed. To him it was like watching *Roots* without understanding that this was a glimpse into a long-ago time before slavery had been abolished.

As they walked out of the theatre, Mike saw the sadness in Julia's face. He hated the idea that although he had meant well, he had exposed Julia to what she saw as confirmation that Americans would not hold open arms out to her. Despite critical acclaim for *Miss Saigon*, which included winning the Olivier Award in London for Best Musical and raves for the current revival, it puzzled and concerned him that Julia found the musical depressing and that it had dampened her self-confidence.

Sitting down for an after-theatre cup of tea and dessert, he reminded Julia that it was only a show, not a documentary. The characters were fictional—made up for dramatic purposes. She should not take the play literally. He also begged her to keep in mind that the action took place in a very different era. The story recounted a tragic romance between a Vietnamese bargirl and an American naval officer who fought in Vietnam during the 1970s. The mood of the play *was* pessimistic. The female Vietnamese protagonist, Kim, has had a child by Chris, the American soldier—their little boy, Tam. Even though a few years have passed, Kim continues to believe that Chris will come back for them, marry her, and take them to America. When Chris returns—with his wife—and asks Kim to give him the boy, Kim feels trapped between cultures. Faced with her heartbreak, and wanting her son to have a better life then she can give him, Kim commits suicide.

To try to revive Julia's spirits, Mike planned another evening that he hoped would create a bond between her and Jennifer, and invited Jason to join them so Julia will have her own "date." To get to their restaurant they walked through Times Square. A world of its own, Times Square—once a seedy mixture of prostitutes and pick-pockets—had over the years been gentrified into a glamorous area fit for families. Enormous digital billboards now illuminated the streets and boulevards, which stretched for several blocks from 42nd to 52nd Streets.

As they headed towards Restaurant Row on West 46th Street, Mike took Jennifer's arm. The two exchanged affectionate glances. Julia could see that their relationship had advanced beyond platonic friendship.

Suddenly Julia asked Jason, "Did you see *Miss Saigon*?"

"Nope," Jason said. "Would love to, though."

"I think it tells the truth," Julia remarked.

Mike's eyes widened. This was the reaction he feared. That production evidently made a lasting negative impression on Julia. "I suggest you not let that play get to you, Julia," he declared. "It was just a story."

"One that happened to many people from Vietnam," Julia retorted.

"True," Jennifer chimed in. "But a lot has happened in the last 45 years. The action in that play took place nearly half a century ago. We've come a long way since then."

Julia shook her head. "Americans like Americans."

"We also like People of other cultures," Jason insisted, trying to lighten her mood. "It's a reason I like you, kiddo."

Julia returned Jason's compliment with a small smile. "You're different."

"So are you. It's what makes us Americans. We respect people for who they are, not where they came from," Jason said.

Julia pressed her argument. "*Miss Saigon* is still real today."

"Baloney," Mike retorted. "You're being unfair to yourself and to the rest of us. That is *not* how most Americans feel."

Concerned with this exchange, Jason was thinking of what else he could say that might put Julia in a better frame of mind. Mike's invitation to join them for the evening had delighted him. Being with Julia outside of acting class felt wonderful, and he really liked her father. He felt like he was floating on air, but Julia was sure in an odd mood. He looked at her. "I'm with your dad. In fact, if Igor ever does put that play on, as he once said he might, you would naturally be perfect to play Kim. Personally I'd say you have the potential to be even better than anyone else."

"Just because of the part of me that's Vietnamese?" she said, but with a sidelong smile, so he would know she was not really offended.

"No. Because of the part of you that's a talented actress."

Julia smiled appreciatively. She liked the fact that Jason always stood up for her. She knew she could count on him. He had proven it by siding with her against Vicky and the others. It had also not escaped her notice when Igor made a comment that Jason just might have the talent of a young Al Pacino. That remark had placed him on a higher level than his classmates.

Igor was always positive and encouraging, but saying that Jason might be the next Pacino—*that* was the real deal. Hearing Igor's comment, Vicky's crowd treated Jason with respect. Partly their attitude was admiration; partly it was political. Who knew when Jason might land a coveted role in a production in which they could be cast? Making him angry was foolish. Thankfully, his harsh criticism of their bullying had eased tensions between Julia and the rest of the class. The snickering had stopped, and Julia's performances had improved significantly.

As they walked along Julia noticed that Jennifer was squeezing Mike's hand and had given him a cooing smile. *Can't you see through her?* Julia wanted to cry out. *The woman just wants you for your money.*

Julia realized she was jealous. But didn't she have the right to be? Her father had promised that he would be with her always. As Julia saw it, that left no room for another woman, especially not *this* one. She conceded to herself that she might level that charge against *any* woman who became involved with her father. Still, she regarded Jennifer, the first woman in whom he had shown serious interest, as a Trojan Horse who threatened the stability of Julia's world.

The group turned onto West 46th Street and headed towards 7th Avenue. Just ahead was Café Roma, known for its outstanding pasta. "Hey guys," Mike said. "I hope everybody's worked up an appetite, because in a couple of minutes you're about to have an opportunity to indulge yourselves." He nodded at Café Roma's sign. "This is where we're going. They are famous for doing the best risotto in New York City."

"I vote for that," Jennifer said.

Mike looked at Jason. "I trust you're in!"

Jason was beaming. "You bet. Thank you! It's really that great?"

"Better," Mike assured him.

Julia responded with a scowl. "I cannot stay for a long dinner. I have to study for class tomorrow. Jason has to study too."

"Aw, come on, spoilsport," Jason kidded. "You're always the most prepared student in class, and tomorrow is a light day."

"Princess, here's the deal," Mike said. "I have Max outside, parked and ready to take us home right after dinner. You can certainly catch a cab if you want to leave a bit earlier, but I think that won't be necessary. It's not going to be a late night."

Julia stopped in the street and just looked at him.

In the uncomfortable silence Jennifer interceded. "Julia, stay as long as you like, but we want your company. It wouldn't be the same without you."

"Fine!" Julia angrily seethed, and charged into the restaurant ahead of them. The three of them followed her, perplexed. A maître'd promptly seated them at a well-situated table for four.

Café Roma was everything Mike had promised. The pasta was Parmigiano-Reggiano, imported from Italy. Too many American parmesans were made with a plant fiber called cellulose. This pasta was hand-cut, and the marinara sauce magnificent. The snapper they all ordered as their main dish was fresh and perfectly roasted, served with the right touch of safflower oil. The only discordant note was Julia's sour attitude. She picked at the food without complimenting it, and sat in stony silence. Jason, in contrast, was at the top of his game. He proved to be a fine raconteur. "How do you drown an actress?" he asked, quoting a joke he had seen on the Internet.

"I give up," Jennifer said. Mike shook his head. Julia just looked at him.

"Put a mirror at the bottom of the pool," Jason said with a straight face. It was an old joke, but Mike and Jennifer burst into laughter while Julia scowled.

"That's a stupid joke. Not every actress is so vain," Julia stated dismissingly.

"Well, who cares!" Jason said. "Here's another one I love. How many actors does it take to screw in a light bulb?" No one knew the answer. "Ten. One to screw in the light and nine to criticize the director for letting the first one grab the spotlight."

After everyone but Julia laughed, Jason looked at her, confused. Her scornful mood was dampening the fun. He hoped to lighten the mood by addressing the elephant in the room. "Julia, what's the deal? Are you upset about something? Did *I* do something to upset you?" he asked plaintively.

When she didn't answer immediately, Mike added his two cents. "Julia, you're behaving like a petulant child."

Firing a fierce look at Jennifer, Julia angrily declared, "Maybe my best friend was stolen from me."

Jennifer gasped.

"Julia!" Mike reprimanded.

Julia got up, stormed out of the restaurant, and went to the curb to hail a taxi back to their Upper East Side penthouse.

Chapter Fifteen

Julia's fiery departure from Café Roma left Mike, Jennifer, and Jason stunned. "Was it something I said?" Jason wondered aloud, his expression sheepish.

Mike looked across at Jennifer. Their eyes met. Both understood intuitively that Julia was acting out this way because of them. Mike realized that Julia was afraid she was losing his affections to another woman. That was the very last thing on Mike's mind. Nothing on the planet could diminish the deep-seated love he had for Julia. She was his daughter and his star. While understanding what motivated Julia, he did not find her conduct appealing or appropriate. There was simply no excuse for how she had been acting lately.

Mike knew he needed a heart-to-heart discussion with Julia. She needed to understand that loving her did not require him to forfeit other aspects of his life. He loved both his daughter and Jennifer. They were just two different kinds of love. Julia needed to take that to heart. He planned to see what Van could do to help. Perhaps she could talk some sense into her granddaughter.

Mike turned to Jason. "Julia hides it well, but she's under a lot of pressure with her studies," he said, trying to excuse his daughter. "Her intensity sometimes gets the better of her."

"Got it," Jason said, relieved. Having developed strong feelings for Julia, the prospect that she could turn on him as she apparently had on Jennifer horrified him.

"Not to worry," Jennifer said, running her hand through her hair. "She likes you, Jason. That's evident."

"You could have fooled me," he commented, but his broad smile

125

betrayed his appreciation of her remark.

"It's all good, my friend," Mike added. "And by the way I am not 'sir.' For you I'm Mike."

"Thank you, sir," Jason said.

The front door of the restaurant opened and Julia returned. She sat down at the table without explanation or apology.

"Hello, stranger!" Mike said, forcing a laugh and trying for a cheerful tone.

"It's raining hard. No taxis," she mumbled.

"Well, we're the lucky ones," Jennifer said. "We love your company."

Julia eyed her without comment. Mike paid and they left. His driver was due any minute, as was the car service he had called to collect Jason and take him back to his Brooklyn apartment. It had begun to pour. They huddled under the restaurant's awning to shield themselves from the driving sheets of rain. The water poured through under the awning and soon everyone was soaked. Jennifer looked at Mike and shrugged. Life was like that. He smiled back. He gave Julia a smile but she stared straight ahead with a sullen expression. The only one she favored with a smile was Jason, as he touched her lightly on the arm. Jason's face brightened. At least she hadn't put him in the dog house. He felt somewhat relieved.

Finally the black Town Car Mike had ordered for Jason arrived and they all bid the young man goodnight. Jason repeated his thanks for the evening. Moments later, Mike's spacious Lincoln pulled up to the curb. Mike ushered Jennifer and Julia into it. Julia got in first. He followed and all three sat in the back, with Mike in the middle. Jennifer and Mike held hands during the journey back to the first stop—her place in SoHo. They all maintained silence during the

20 minute ride, but Jennifer smiled at Mike. He touched her on the nose, lovingly.

Julia winced when Jennifer rested her head against his shoulder. There was heavy traffic and the going was slow. The air in the car was tense. Everybody was uncomfortable. Finally Mike asked Max, his driver, to turn on the radio. Max hit the knob and the car filled their ears with the grand sounds of Beethoven's *Symphony Number 9 in D minor, Opus 125*. The uplifting music made the ride a bit more bearable.

The car finally reached Jennifer's gallery and apartment, and Max parked the car at the curb.

"Would you like to come inside?" Jennifer asked. "I can make us tea. I have all kinds—Earl Gray, peppermint, blueberry—you name it."

"That sounds like a great idea," Mike exclaimed. "Julia?"

Julia nodded reluctantly and they went inside. She was curious to see what the apartment looked like. It was a one bedroom—about a thousand square feet. One thing Julia was forced to acknowledge was that Jennifer had good taste. The polished wood floor was covered with Turkish rugs. These included a combination of Halis, Kilims, and Sumaks. The chairs were covered with tapestry fabrics. Golden silk covered a luxurious sofa. The art on her walls was worthy of her gallery: a combination of paintings from up-and-coming New York artists. Her kitchen was compact and efficient, like a ship's galley, with appliances made of polished steel. Jennifer took pride in explaining the artists she had chosen to grace her walls.

Mike and Jennifer had Earl Gray while Julia opted for peppermint.

"Don't you see yourself on stage soon?" Jennifer asked.

"Maybe," Julia replied. "My teacher, Igor, says I have talent, but I think luck has a lot to do with it."

"But talent counts the most, and you have it," Mike said.

"I worry about my English," Julia confided. She was trying to be pleasant, and after all they *were* talking about her!

"Mike says it is improving all the time," Jennifer said encouragingly.

Julia studied Jennifer carefully. On this topic she seemed sincere. She still thought her constant touching of her father was too studied. She decided that women like Jennifer could be likeable and charming as well as calculating. The prospect of her monopolizing her father made her anxious. She could see that he was falling for Jennifer. He made no effort to conceal the fact. What could *she* do about it?

As Mike and Julia left and were settled into the back seat of their limo, Mike remarked, "She's a good woman, Julia. Cut her some slack. She's funny, smart, and she knows where to find the best croissants in New York. I like her."

"I can see that," Julia said sarcastically.

Mike gave her a look as the car moved back into the heavy night-time traffic. "You've got to give people an opportunity, Princess. Jennifer likes you. Why can't you be friends?"

"She's a gold-digger! Julia snapped.

Mike drew a breath. "How can you say that? You barely know her."

"She wants what you have, not you."

Her father's expression betrayed his exasperation. "Julia, I don't know where all this is coming from. She has her own money and it's the least of her concerns. Anyway, I didn't get where I am by being a poor judge of character. Don't I deserve some credit? You really don't have to protect, me, you know!"

"Love blinds people," Julia remarked. She hated herself for say-ing it but there was no resisting the impulse. Jennifer was a threat to her relationship with her father. Julia was determined to shield him. There was no way she would let the woman sink her claws into her father. Her father had suffered too much with the loss of her mother. He didn't need Jennifer. He had her. *Wasn't that enough?*

"Julia, you disappoint me."

Julia turned her face away from Mike and leaned her head against the glass window. The memory of her mother returned. She remembered her mother's beauty and the rich fragrances that graced her body. The contrast between PH and Jennifer was stark. PH represented good in the world. Julia remembered the power of her mother's love for her father and how deeply he had returned her love. In loving Jennifer, it felt like he was betraying the memory of her mother.

Mike saw a tear streaming down Julia's face. He clasped her arm. "Darling, what's wrong? I'm your father. You can tell me. No secrets between us. Isn't that what we promised each other?"

Julia faced him, her eyes moist. "I'm sorry, papa, it's just that sometimes I miss mother so much. Yes, even now after all this time." Sharing her pain, Mike embraced her. In his arms, her fears vanished, like a bad dream. She snuggled close to her father and held on tightly as he gently stroked her hair.

Chapter Sixteen

The theatre lights darkened and the spotlight was on the character of Tracy Lord, the main protagonist in *The Philadelphia Story*. Igor had assigned the leading role to Julia as a sign of his confidence that Julia was doing better with English. Tracy was a challenging part. John Barry's strength as a comedic writer lay in his gift for writing witty repartee. The play was written specifically for Katherine Hepburn, who used the play, when it opened on Broadway, as a vehicle to establish her stardom once and for all. *Holiday* had been a hit but *The Philadelphia Story* made her reputation. Hepburn later purchased the film rights and got Cary Grant to co-star with her.

John Barry's play is about repartee and timing. It was ideal for teaching. Observing the rapport that had developed between Julia and Jason, he assigned Jason the role of Dexter, Tracy's estranged husband, with whom Tracy remained in love. Their chemistry translated well for stage presence. Barry's pithy language offered Julia an ideal opportunity to show off her English skills.

Igor admired Julia's perseverance. He felt sure she would come through with flying colors. He knew that when Julia wasn't looking her jealous classmates sniped. He hoped that giving Julia scenes in which she could shine would mute their mean-spirits.

The students had been working hard for several months. Igor believed it was time to test their resolution and ambition. Casting directors sought his recommendations. Hank Strong and Cecilia Morehouse were each starring in hit Broadway productions. Both had started off as his students. His recommendation got them cast in roles that the *New York Times* predicted would win them Tony nominations. Everyone in the class knew the stakes. It ratcheted up the competitive tensions.

Igor had cautioned students to prepare for rehearsals. He reminded them that their craft looked easy only from a distance, and only to outsiders. Auditions required actors to hit their marks and know their lines. Top professionals always rehearsed carefully for what appeared to be casual moves.

The dynamic injected fierce competition. Actors have fragile egos. Casting directors, critics, and audiences would applaud well-turned performances, but they would pounce on any mistake. Julia practiced her lines with her regular acting partner and friend, Bethany, a University of Michigan graduate, who had made her way to New York hoping for her big break. They had met at a previous acting class and Julia had convinced her to join Igor's class. Like Julia, Bethany was finding the craft challenging. Igor gave her the role of Liz Imbrie, a journalist sent to cover Tracy's upcoming wedding.

For this student production, Igor let the cast wear their own clothes. He had persuaded a set designer to dress the stage. The sides of dialogue were set on the porch in front of the library in Tracy's mansion. Julia began to speak as she turned to Jason. Tracy, planning to marry another man, remains unable to grasp that while having cast off Dexter for heavy drinking, he remained the only man in her heart. Hepburn and Grant had brought the characters vividly to life.

Julia had spent the last twenty-four hours memorizing her lines. The role of Tracy appealed to her. She was a woman she could identify with—a woman in search of herself. Tracy is not sure what she really wants or how to achieve it.

Of course Julia *did* know what she wanted: her father's love and acceptance by her peers. But Tracy's search for love echoed her own. Tracy's intense love for Dexter, which she finally admits to herself, echoed her own feelings for her father.

As the lights dimmed she felt her stomach tighten and her throat go dry. Momentarily she lost the thread of Barry's text, but as the music ended, she got a grip on herself and the lines were right there.

Dexter—Jason— appeared on stage. "Hello," he said.

As Tracy, Julia met his eyes firmly. Her body language expressed Tracy's skepticism and her attraction to Dexter. "Fancy seeing you here," he said, crossing to his right. Both Jason and Julia had an instinctive sense of how to employ body movement to express character.

"Orange juice?" Jason asked, pouring two glasses.

"You're sure you don't want something stronger? I'll ring if you like," Julia tempted him, testing. She sat on a stool and waited for his response.

"Not now, thanks," Dexter told Tracy. "This juice is fine."

"Don't tell me you've forsaken your beloved whiskey-and-whiskies." Julia captured the arch quality of Tracy's patrician character. An audience could easily discern her accent, but Julia's panache carried her. Tracy would tread where angels feared to go. Igor nodded approvingly.

"No, indeed," Jason replied. "I've just changed their color, that's all. I go in for the pale pastel shades now—like this juice." He held up his glass. "I find they're more becoming."

"Dexter, would you mind doing something for me?" Tracy asked.

"Anything—what?" Jason embodied Dexter's debonair mannerism.

"Get the hell out of here!" Julia snapped, with perfect timing. Out of the corner of her eye she caught Igor grinning. So were her classmates, even Vicky and Linda.

"Oh, no, I couldn't do that," Dexter said. "That wouldn't be fair to you. You need me too much."

Julia related to the words. She wanted Mike to mouth the same words to her. She lifted her nose. "Would you mind telling me just what it is you're hanging around for?"

Jason started to move off-stage.

Julia raised a palm. "No—please don't go! I'd honestly much prefer it if you wouldn't." Julia felt shaky but good. Igor nodded encouragement. Everyone had the text of the play and was following closely, locked and loaded for the opportunity to comment on any slip. They reminded her of crocodiles eyeing their next meal. She could sense the jaws snapping open and shut in hungry anticipation.

"So should I," Dexter said. "Honestly, you never looked better in your life. You're getting a fine, tawny look...."

Julia reached for the next line. She froze. Her tongue felt like something was clamping on it.

In unison, Vicky and Linda called out the next line, "Oh, we're going to talk about me, aren't we? Goody!" The class burst out in laughter and sneered.

"Class, be professional!" Igor snapped. He turned to Julia and beckoned her to proceed. "Julia, do you need to check the text?"

"No, Igor, I think I remember," she replied. She eyed Bethany, who behaved generously, giving her a thumbs-up sign. Julia smiled back and nodded at Igor.

"Ready," Julia said. She continued, and got the lines wrong. Instead of sounding like a Philadelphia socialite, she sounded like an Asian servant girl.

"What interests me is what, if anything, your real scheme is," Julia continued. When she said "scheme" it came out sounding more like *sweem*. Julia hunched her shoulders, and appreciated what actors meant by "stage fright."

134

"It's scheme," Linda called out "*Sweem?* That's a bird call." She lifted her head like a magpie. "*Sweem, Sweem,*" she chirped. Vicky snickered at Linda's sarcasm.

Julia looked at Igor helplessly. "I'm sorry, Igor. I thought I had it."

Igor stood up and turned to the class reproachfully. "Class, you may be heaping scorn on one of your classmates today, but remember that every actor stands on the cliff's edge. I expect support, not criticism." He shot Linda and Vicky nasty looks. "That means the two of you."

Julia saw Jason clench his fist, urging her to stay strong. He had often expressed his attitude in familiar American slang: *When you're going through hell, keep going.* Julia knew that was a sensible perspective, but the cackling led by Vicky sent tears streaming down her face. Julia rushed off-stage and slumped into a chair.

Igor went to her, and calmed her down with a gentle reminder. "Julia, you should know your lines. Always be prepared."

"I did know my lines," she said. "I don't know why I went blank, Igor. I just don't know." She felt ashamed and confused.

Igor softened his tone. "Every actor falls into that pit. Every single one of us. You're not alone."

"No, but it's also my English. I can't get it right."

"No," Igor corrected. "Barry's language is elegant, but getting it right requires focus. You can do this. Now stop feeling sorry for yourself. Be the star I know you are."

"You really believe I'm that good?" Julia asked, needing his reassurance.

"Without question," Igor nodded.

Julia got up and they resumed the scene. This time Julia was able to get through the words. Her elocution was reasonable, if imperfect.

After the exercise, Igor led the class through a detailed critique and praised Julia and Bethany. He went out of his way to boost Julia's ego.

Julia appreciated Igor's support. Jason came and hugged her. He reminded her of how he had blown half his lines during a scene from *West Side Story*. Jason's consolation helped. Still, a big part of Julia's challenge lay in her inability to enunciate.

Class concluded and everyone made for the door. As Julia, Bethany, and Jason were leaving the theatre, they found Vicky and Linda lounging against the building's brick wall. Neither deigned to speak directly to Julia. Instead they talked loudly, making sure that Julia could hear every word. "I wish I had a rich daddy like her," Vicky sniped. "Maybe he could buy me a theatre *and* a theatre company."

"It's good to be a daddy's girl." Linda added.

As she and Jason reached the bottom of the steps and other students streamed by, Julia turned around and slapped Vicky on the cheek. It was a hard slap that left a stinging red mark on the blonde's face. Vicky howled in pain. "Why you little bitch!" Vicky exclaimed, holding her hand to her reddened face.

Jason stepped between the girls. "Hey, guys, knock it off," he shouted.

"Sure, stand up for your spoiled brat girlfriend," Linda jabbed, as Vicky rubbed her reddened cheek.

"You're a sniveling little no talent, Linda. You too Vicky," Jason retorted. "You're assholes. Both of you." He paused as if to consider a point, then eyed them. "On second thought, you know what—I get your jealousy. I don't blame you. You'll both spend your entire lives waiting tables while Julia opens under the great white lights."

Jason's harsh jabs jolted the two girls. A silence passed between all of them. Abruptly Vicky said, "Hey, wait Jason, we weren't trying to be mean about it…."

"You weren't trying. You just *were*." He glared. "You two are made from the same mold," he added. "You want to do something useful for your future? Figure out if you want to wait tables in a bar or a Starbucks."

Jason turned to Julia and placed his arm around her.

"Sorry for these two idiots. Ignore them," he said. "Are you okay?"

"I am fine. Thanks, Jason. You have a good heart."

"They were making fun of my papa." Her voice had become somber.

Jason shrugged. "People made fun of my parents too."

"Really? What happened?"

"There was this kid, Robbie."

"Uh huh."

"He said something about us being poor because my mom was shopping at the Dollar Store."

"What did you do?"

"I punched him in the face. He never said anything about me or my family after that."

"Jason," she said, a smile crossing her face, "in case I didn't say it before, you're a great friend."

"I love you, too," he smiled, clasping her arm affectionately. Then he said, "Now you listen to me."

"Listening," Julie said, a bright expression on her face.

"You're better than they are."

"How can you be certain?" she said.

"I learned from your father," he said.

"Good person to learn from," she beamed. "My papa is the greatest."

"You said it, babe," Jason said.

"I like the way you think," she said.

"It gets better," he intoned.

"Yeah?"

"Definitely."

"How do I find out more?"

He lifted an eyebrow. "Ah, you want to know my secrets."

"Secrets are fun to know."

"Then you'll just have to stick with me to find out."

She pretended to be outraged. "Now you *are* teasing me."

"Yes," he said proudly. "You are so much fun to tease."

She pondered his words for a minute. She didn't always like being teased but Jason made it fun. He made her feel more at ease. More normal. More like somebody who fit into a culture.

"You are a silly boy," she tried to tease back.

He made a funny face and she laughed.

"You are A-O-K, Mr. Jason!" she said.

"Now there you go," he said. "That's the ticket. Keep that up and tomorrow you'll sound just like a home girl."

"Home girl," she grinned. "I like it. Me. Home girl."

"My girl," Jason declared. He smiled wistfully.

He checked his watch. "Look, got to bop. Check you later, kid-do." She smiled as he turned and walked down the street.

Then, checking her watch, she frowned. *Where was papa?* she wondered. He should have been here by now.

Chapter Seventeen

A horn sounded behind Julia. She turned as her father's driver pulled up. Mike was in the back seat waving to Julia. She moved towards him, eager to see her father but troubled by the day's events. Then she saw Jennifer seated beside him.

"No, no, no, no" she screamed to herself.

"Julia!" Mike called out cheerfully. Julia noticed that Jennifer was gripping Mike's hand.

"Hi Julia," Jennifer said amicably. "How are you?"

"Ok. I'm fine." Her eyes shifted to her father.

"Hop in," Mike said. "I've got great news."

Julia gave him a skeptical look. For her there was no such thing as great news when Jennifer was involved. "What?" she uttered as Mike opened the car door for Julia.

"Jennifer is making bouillabaisse for dinner. For you, grandma and me. It's her specialty."

Jennifer leaned over Mike and asked Julia, "Have you ever had bouillabaisse?"

Julie didn't bother answering. She sat in stony silence, looking out the window as if she had not heard the question addressed to her.

Jennifer went on as if Julia had answered: "It's a traditional Provencal fish stew. It originated in Marseille. The French make it with mussels, turbot and monkfish, although I'm using lobster. The herbs and vegetables give it a distinctive quality. I'm making it just for you guys."

Julia eyed Jennifer and Mike.

"Come on, Julia," Mike said. "At least be a sport about it."

"Sure, okay," she said grudgingly, not wanting to get her father upset.

Jennifer relaxed. "I promise you'll find this is a real treat."

Soon enough they arrived at Mike's Fifth Avenue high rise. Once upstairs, Jennifer donned an apron and commandeered the kitchen. Van was happy to help, and Jennifer put her to work chopping vegetables. Van appreciated fine cuisine and was fascinated to learn. Mike acted as scullery maid, cleaning the pots, pans, and knives.

Jennifer prepared her dish meticulously. She heated the oven and arranged bread slices in a baking pan, then brushed both sides with oil. When the bread was done she rubbed each side with a cut garlic clove. The soup was complicated. She cooked the lobster, removed the meat and reserved the juices. She cooked the tomatoes, onion, and garlic. She cut potatoes into half inch cubes. She added fennel fronds, bay leaf, saffron, sea salt, and pepper, then broth, and finally fish, then let the mixture simmer.

Julia grew bored. Papa was clearly bewitched by this woman, but she didn't have to stay and watch them interact. It was just too painful. She turned abruptly, without a word, and walked down the hall to her bedroom.

Jennifer looked at Mike as Julia disappeared.

"Was it something I said?" she wondered, unsettled.

"She's hard to get to know," Mike said. He looked at Van for support.

"You did nothing wrong, Jennifer," Van agreed. "Give Julia time. She'll come around."

"I do hope so, because I really like and admire her," Jennifer said, turning up the heat on the broth. She picked up a wooden spoon, stirred the broth, and tasted it. She nodded approvingly, dipped the spoon and offered Van and Mike tastes. Both their faces lit up.

"As a Frenchman, I confess, my homeland created the greatest cuisine on the planet."

Van gave him a playful slap on the shoulder. "You keep telling us that."

"Well, this dish certainly qualifies," Jennifer smiled. She turned her head towards Julia's bedroom, her expression betraying a note of anxiety.

Behind the closed door, Julia peered closely at her computer screen, having Googled Julia's name. Sherlock Holmes would have envied Julia's concentration as she searched the Internet for evidence that would crack the case against Jennifer. Who *was* Jennifer Robson?

Jennifer's website was a treasure-trove of information. Jennifer hailed from Cleveland, and had spent time in London in the art world. To Julia that meant she had a humble beginning, so her fancy airs must have been carefully constructed. She had to admit that Jennifer had made her business a success—and of course she was not shy boasting about all her accomplishments. Her website highlighted reviews from the *New York Times* art section and several art journals. One review epitomized the consensus: *"Ms. Robson is a stylish curator. Her select clientele knows they can trust her judgment on art. When she says something is right, you can take that to the bank. It's called integrity—a quality that isn't as common in the high stakes of international art."*

Julia checked Jennifer's Facebook page. One entry caught her eye and made her feel so light-headed she was sure she was going to faint. There it was: Jennifer wrote that she had a very special new man in her life and that he loved her taste in croissants. She went on to say she had high hopes that this was 'The One' she had been waiting for her whole life, and that she was "determined to do everything she could to make it work!" This was Julia's father she was talking about! Determined to do everything she could? Yes, rope him in, get his money for herself, and leave him a bitter, broken man.

"Well, not if I can help it, Jennifer," she vowed aloud. "You have met your match."

Chapter Eighteen

Returning from her computer search, Julia sat down at the dinner table with Jennifer, Mike, and Van. She seethed, wanting to accuse Jennifer of being a gold digger. But she needed solid evidence. In the meantime she played the game, and praised Jennifer on her bouillabaisse. Jennifer beamed with pride.

Julia tried to think objectively. Did she selfishly want to deny her father the company of another person who made him happy? Julia realized that emotions cloud judgments. *Any* woman who came into her father's life meant danger to her relationship with her beloved Papa. But Jennifer was a real threat.

First, Jennifer was a Westerner, so different from her exotic mother, and of course from Julia herself. Jennifer's playfulness, business achievements, and intelligent conversation attracted Mike. Even her grandmother seemed to like the woman. Julia also thought about Jennifer's well-done website, well-decorated apartment, and serious cooking skills. It all looked fine. It was all so perfect. Perhaps too perfect? Anyone who presented a picture of perfection was spinning an illusion. Julia trusted her own instincts. *She had to protect her Papa.* She would sacrifice her life for him. She would rid their lives of this unwelcome intrusion.

According to the news accounts Julia had read on the Internet, Jennifer had exposed brokers who attempted to palm off fake Picassos or Pollacks. Her reputation for exposing counterfeits had flowered. To Julia the art dealer herself was a fake. Julia resolved to devise a plan to rid Jennifer from their lives.

The next afternoon, Julia rang Jennifer, who was in the kitchen putting out a small bowl of food for her silver-furred Persian cat, Jasper. She answered after the second ring.

"Jennifer?"

"Yes?"

"This is Julia."

"Oh, Julia—what a pleasant surprise. Nice hearing your voice again."

"Thank you, Jennifer. I called to thank you for that delicious dinner."

"Julia, it was my pleasure."

"I've been rude to you."

Jennifer laughed. "Julia, thank you, but really, it can take a while to know another person. I'm hoping we can become great friends. We're both, in our own way, involved in the world of art. Mine involves oil on canvas while yours involves acting and performance." Jennifer was exuberant. Perhaps she had misjudged Mike's ice-queen daughter.

"I'd like us to be friends too," Julia said encouragingly.

"I have some other dishes I think you might enjoy."

"Good Jennifer. I can't wait. Um, Jennifer, I also called because I have a personal favor to ask."

"Anything."

"I have to buy my father a tie at Bergdorf's. You have good taste. Can we select it together? Today?"

"Absolutely," Jennifer said. They agreed to meet outside the store, located on Fifth Avenue and 57th Street, at 2:00. Julia hung up and smiled mischievously. "Let's see how composed and charming she is when her feathers are ruffled. She'll lose her cool and my father will see her true colors," she thought.

****

After hanging up, Jennifer assigned a client interested in a Renoir print to an assistant and went upstairs to check her appearance. She wanted to dress comfortably and perhaps more casually, with nice wool slacks and a cashmere sweater. Something in her said that Julia, as a person in the acting profession, might be subconsciously wary of people she thought were too polished. She felt sure she just needed to understand Julia better. She changed, then grabbed her coat and gloves and strode out onto the chilly Manhattan streets.

An hour later, Jennifer found herself standing alone outside the front entrance to the Bergdorf's, freezing despite her warm outerwear. She checked her Tiffany platinum watch every ten minutes. Julia was more than reasonably late. Jennifer passed more time gazing at the window displays. At 3:30, with no sign of Mike's daughter, she called Julia, but got only voicemail. She texted her. Fifteen minutes later she called again. She got another voicemail. Finally, at 4:00 sharp, Jennifer accepted that Julia had deliberately stood her up.

Such behavior was unacceptable. Julia was a young woman, not a child. *"Spoiled brat,"* Jennifer mumbled as she trudged back to work. Julia didn't have to like her, but showing respect was only polite. She decided to tell Mike. His reaction might determine the course of their relationship.

Chapter Nineteen

"What in the world has gotten into you? Jennifer was waiting for you in the cold for almost two hours!" Mike shouted as he eyed Julia across the table. "Where do you get off treating *anyone* so rudely, let alone someone you know I really like? Jennifer is running a business. She left an important client in the hands of an assistant because—listen to me Julia, listen carefully—because she *likes* you and you flattered her by asking her to help select a tie for me." He paused. "What were you thinking?"

They were facing off in the kitchen. Van was sitting at the table, sipping tea and listening closely. Julia's behavior was definitely out of character.

Julia batted her eyelashes innocently. "I don't know, papa," she said, apathetically. "I suppose I acted on impulse, then just forgot about it."

Mike rubbed his face. "Impulse?" His voice cracked like a whip. "Impulse means lack of control. Lack of discipline. All from a young lady who is showing genuine discipline professionally. I'm not buying that. Level with me, Julia. What is going through your mind? I will not stand for your mistreating Jennifer. She has gone out of her way to be gracious. She shows you every courtesy." He leaned towards his daughter. "I like this woman. Wreck my relationship with her and I will not be happy. Do we understand one another?"

Mike's anger took Julia aback. She was used to her father leaning over backwards to reassure her that, whatever happened, things would be all right between them. A shudder of fear convulsed her.

In trying to protect her father, she might be separating herself from him.

"I'm sorry, papa," she said, tears welling up. "I was wrong."

"Not good enough," Mike said, refusing to let her off the hook. "You owe Jennifer a sincere apology. Make it right."

"I will," Julia promised. She trodded out of the kitchen. Van motioned to Mike to sit down, and brought him a cup of her brewed tea. "Please, Mike, calm down." He did but his facial expression showed how upset he felt.

"There's no excuse for how Julia is acting around Jennifer," Van said, "but go easy. This is a very difficult time. You have some responsibility here."

"I know, Van. I know now that when I took Julia all over the world with me, traveling for business, it denied her the chance to develop deep friendships. It was always the two of us against the world. But she's not a little girl anymore and Jennifer is now in my life. This is my chance for love again, for happiness. I may not get another chance."

Van was sympathetic. "Yes. You deserve happiness Mike. She will come around. She just has to get used to the idea that she has to share you with another woman."

Mike was not mollified. "Let's hope she can adapt. If she can't accept Jennifer then we don't need to live in the same house."

Van looked stricken. "Mike, you would throw your own daughter out the door?"

Mike drew a breath. "No, Van, no one is ejecting Julia. I would move out. I feel she's leaving me no choice." Van's eyes widened as he continued. "Talk to her, Van, for all our sakes."

Van's face went white. There was no mistaking Mike's tone. Julia had pushed him too far.

Mike stormed out of the kitchen. In seconds Van heard the door to his office study slam shut.

Moments later Julia sees that Mike was no longer in the room and crept back into the kitchen. Wordlessly Julia searched Van's eyes, seeking support. Van looked at her cautiously. Abruptly, she said, "Like it or not, Julia, Jennifer is now part of your father's life. I have never seen him so upset. He has threatened to move out unless you stop being disrespectful."

"Grandma, he would do that? He would leave us—*me*—for Jennifer?"

"He would." Van took a breath. She hated saying these things but someone had to level with her granddaughter. "You have hurt him badly."

"Grandma, Jennifer is no good for him," Julia protested.

"Who are you to say that? On what evidence? She has been pleasant to all of us, including you, no matter how badly you acted."

"I just feel it," Julia sulked in reply.

"You *feel* it? Child, name a single thing Jennifer has done that justifies that conclusion?" Julia had no answer.

"Do you really think papa would leave us?" she wondered, weakly.

"Yes," Van stated firmly. "You've turned him into a tempest of emotions. Tempests are unpredictable. And they can inflict great damage." She came over and clasped Julia. "Granddaughter, I love you as I loved my own daughter. You are my flesh and blood. But I have a duty to protect you *and* your father."

"Thank you, grandma," Julia said, close to tears. She saw how idiotic her impulsive gambit had been.

Abruptly, Julia experienced a flashback: the image of little Julia in a hotel room with her father. She was sprawled on the bed happily working on one of her coloring books while her father spoke on the phone. It was a delicious memory. They had spent years traveling together. The places they saw were strange and exotic. Sharing these experiences with her father made each one fresh and exciting. Life without Mike was unimaginable.

A new image flashed through her mind. Her mother was cuddling with her. She was singing a lullaby to Julia. PH had made Julia feel secure. She knew who she was. She understood what she wanted to be. Her mother's death had thrown everything off balance. Julia found her perspective distorted. She was struggling to deal with that reality in all its dimensions. Yet every time she seemed close to mastering the challenge, it changed shape again, vanishing like a ghost.

Sometimes she even thought she heard voices taunting her— telling her she was a half-person, half Vietnamese, half American, and not fully anything. At those times, the only comfort she got was looking in the mirror. Not because she was vain: she knew people thought she was beautiful. For her, the value of her beauty was how closely she resembled her mother. Jolted by what was unfolding, Julia became contrite. "You're right, grandma. I must do better, and I will."

Van hugged her granddaughter, hoping that her confusion and jealousy would disappear. It had to, she thought, lest it destroy everything that mattered in her life.

Chapter Twenty

"How the hell did I find you?" Mike asked. He gave Jennifer a wistful look. They were seated inside a booth in a smoky bar in Greenwich Village. A jazz pianist was playing. The place was half full, enough to inject life into the bar. But the crowd would not be packed until late at night. For now Mike and Jennifer could easily hear each other's conversation.

"I was the prize at the bottom of that Crackerjacks box you bought at the Yankees game," she laughed.

He humorously pretended to engage in deep thinking and nodded thoughtfully. "Yeah, that was it. I knew there was something funny going on. The woman who sold it to me had angel's wings."

"My emissaries are everywhere," Jennifer grinned.

"Well, I know one thing."

"Yes?" she said teasingly.

"You found me."

"No," she responded. "You found me." She rested her head back. "In the eighteenth century, there was a view about love. It was that lovers were fated—that specific people were meant for one another. I always thought there was a lot of truth to that."

Mike cocked an eye. "Are you saying we're meant for each other?"

"Is that a serious question?"

"What—you want every mystery unraveled?"

"You bet."

"Life is tough."

"That's not fair."

"Neither is life." He leaned over and kissed her lightly.

Afterwards they strolled hand-in-hand through the Village and back to SoHo. It was early evening. A golden sun still illuminated a deep blue sky. Perhaps fortune was smiling upon them. The signs had grown more fortuitous. Jennifer had received a voice mail from Julia as well as a deeply apologetic text message. Jennifer had glowed as she showed it to Mike. His face beamed with relief.

Julia had texted: *Jennifer. I am sorry for my behavior. This time I mean it. Can you please come to our house for dinner tonight? Grandma and I are making it specially for you. We don't do bouillabaisse, but Vietnam has splendid delicacies that equal the finest cuisine anywhere. Please say yes and let us be friends.*

Emotion choked Jennifer's voice. "Do you think we've turned the corner?"

Mike studied the message. Apparently his straight talk had hit the mark. Her apology indicated that she was measuring up to his confidence in her. "Tonight should be wonderful," he said, and drew Jennifer to him for a long, deeply felt kiss.

Chapter Twenty One

In addition to the dinner Julia had scheduled, she had carefully selected a bouquet of flowers. Julia has chosen well: white roses for purity and tradition, yellow roses for friendship, and blue hydrangeas to suggest a touch of peace and harmony.

Jennifer arrived in a simple white dress accented with a gold chain. Mike was dashing in a dark suit, blue silk shirt, and no tie. Julia wore a long blue dress that fit her like a glove and showed off her lithe figure. It was a lovely Vietnamese garment that had belonged to her mother. In it she especially resembled Phuong Ha at her loveliest. She had worn her hair down, and placed a rose in it to add a touch of soft femininity. Van was wearing an elegant purple dress with gold embroidery. This evening she was carrying a cane, as lately she had been a bit unsteady on her feet. Mike and Julia had urged her to see her doctor, but, stubbornly, she kept putting it off.

The mood was festive as Mike popped a bottle of Tattinger champagne and poured the bubbly into Tiffany flutes. They toasted each other's good health and hope for long lives of health and prosperity. Jennifer was overcome by Julia's new warmth. She flattered Julia on her appearance and asked about her theatre classes.

"Igor is holding a class audition. He's casting us for a Shakespearean drama," Julia reported.

"That sounds great. Which one?" Jennifer asked.

"Not sure yet. I'm guessing *Hamlet*."

"Wow, Shakespeare. He must have confidence. How's your English? You sound much more relaxed with it."

"I am," Julia nodded. Her eyelids fluttered. "I've studied hard."

"That's my Julia," Mike proclaimed. He gave Julia a hug. He drew back and pointed to her. "Ladies, I don't know about you, but I think we've got ourselves a budding star."

"Hear, Hear!" Jennifer cried out, raising her glass.

"A star!" Van agreed, clinking her glass with Jennifer's.

"I still worry about my accent," Julia confessed.

"Don't," Mike reassured her. "You're going to master all your lessons. Don't let anyone tell you differently."

Van ushered everyone to the dining table. She and Julia had spent a good part of the day cooking fine Vietnamese dishes. Tonight they served *Pho bo,* Vietnam's national dish. It consisted of steaming aromatic beef broth served in a deep bowl. Thin slices of beef, tender rice noodles and tasty herbs give it a special flavor. Other items included *Goi cuon,* in which pork, shrimp, rice, vermicelli, mind and beet sprouts are wrapped in thin rice paper discs softened in hot water. *Banh xeo*—crepes filled with shrimp, lettuce, and herbs dipped in sauce—completed the mouth-watering array. *Che,* a form of rice pudding, had been prepared for dessert.

"Everything is delicious," Jennifer told Julia and Van. "Please text me the recipes, would you? I'd love to have them."

Van smiled. "I'm glad you liked the Pho Bo. It was my mother's recipe." Julia nodded graciously and they all rose and retired to the living room. Eventually the talk shifted to theatre.

"*Hamlet,* eh?" Jennifer said. "Why do you think Igor might choose that play? Why not *Macbeth*?"

Julia and the class had debated that idea. Jason, who had a nose for these things, was predicting that Igor would select *Hamlet* for their closing student production. Julia had her money on *Macbeth.* She looked up. "*Macbeth* is about ambition and treachery. Shakespeare wrote about a man who changes from good to evil. As the play opens, he is a hero. Knowing that he can be king twists his mind. His wife, Lady Macbeth, is even more ambitious. She wants him to be king so badly that she pressures him to commit murder. His descent into insanity makes us sympathetic to him, but then he loses our sympathy after he murders his friend Banquo. I love the intense drama!"

Julie looked at all of them, as they hung on her every word, impressed. "Shakespeare created a roller coaster of emotions," she continued. "Macbeth's own actions cause his downfall. Hamlet is even more interesting. He, too, causes his own downfall. He's haunted by his father's death because it is his uncle who killed his father, and then marries his mother, Gertrude. That drives him mad. He sees his father's ghost and speaks to him, promising revenge. He wants to die, yet he feels he needs to take revenge. In the process, he destroys Ophelia, who loves him passionately. He rejects her and she kills herself. While Macbeth's tragic flaw is his ambition, Hamlet's is his quest for revenge."

She paused, then concluded her descriptions. "They are both great plays. I personally prefer Hamlet." What she did not say was how closely she identified with Hamlet at times. Like Hamlet, she heard ghostly voices that mocked her. She sometimes felt being driven mad by her obsessive love for her father.

"Wow, Julia," Jennifer nodded, "You know a lot." She looked at Mike, who leaned across the table and said, "Julia, I knew you were on top of this. My compliments on a thorough analysis of both plays. If Igor decides on *Hamlet* do you think he'll select you for Ophelia?"

"Don't know," Julia said. "We never know what he will do. Both Vicky and her friend Linda want the role. Jason says I'm the best. I don't know about my accent for that part. The part of Ophelia has a lot of lines."

"Persevere, believe in yourself, and you can't fail," Jennifer declared.

Julia's eyes met Jennifer's. "Thank you. I do want the role. But now, please, Jennifer, tell me about you. How did you come to New York?"

Jennifer was happy to talk about herself. She had hoped that Julia would provide her an opportunity to do so. "Well, I lived in London for a stretch, as an art broker. I dealt with brokers from Berlin to Rome, Paris to Tokyo." She paused. "I was seeing someone there. It didn't work out. London can be a lonely place in that situation. I decided it was time to move home to New York."

"Ah, I see," Julia said politely. She turned to Van, and in Vietnamese said, in a harsh tone: *"You see. She's had a few boyfriends. She just looks for the right ones. Now she wants papa!"*

Van, in shock at this turn of events, forced a smile, as if Julia had said something flattering, but her words back in their native tongue were blunt. *"Stop it, Julia. You are going back to your very bad behavior. You are impolite. Jennifer is single. Why shouldn't she have boyfriends?"*

Julia shrugged. *"I'm just saying."*

Van's smile grew brighter. She was extremely uncomfortable. She looked at Jennifer. "Julia thinks it's difficult to move from one foreign culture to another."

"I don't trust anything she says," Julia advised Van in Vietnamese.

"Speak English, Julia," Mike interjected. "We all want to hear what you have to say."

Julia affected a smile. "Thank you, Papa. And I did not mean to be rude." She turned to Jennifer. "What do you know about my mom?"

The change of topic confused Jennifer, but she forced herself to smile. "I know she was a big star, a wonderful singer and actress, and had many fans who adored her. She was beautiful—like you, Julia." She held Julia's gaze. "She made your father proud. I can see why he loved her." She smiled at Mike, who nodded appreciatively.

He looked at the dress that Julia was wearing. "I notice that was your mom's."

"Yes," Julia said. "It is mother's dress. It fits me perfectly. I look a lot like her, don't I, father?"

"Yes, Julia, you do." Mike said quietly, alarmed at the direction in which this conversation was going.

Julia turned to Jennifer. "So, Jennifer, you were an art dealer in London?" While the questions seemed innocent, she spoke with the tone of a prosecuting attorney.

"Yes," Jennifer affirmed, confused.

"Uh huh. You liked it?"

"The work was stimulating. I like what I do. In fact, I love it."

Their eyes were locked together. Jennifer tensed. Julia shot her a stern look. "You make a lot of money?"

"Julia!" Mike exclaimed. "That's rude. You do not ask people questions like that."

Julia ignored her father and looked at Van. In Vietnamese, she declared, *"Like I said, she just wants papa's money."*

Van ignored Julia and smiled at Jennifer. "When something thrills her, Julia often lapses into Vietnamese. She thinks it's wonderful that you appreciate art."

Julia's eyes blazed. "That is *not* what I said," she hissed in English. "Admit it, Jennifer. You don't love my papa. You just want his money. It's all about that, isn't it? Getting your hands on his bank account and living in a grand house like this?"

Mike glared. "Dammit, Julia, what in the world is wrong with you?" He cast an eye at Jennifer. She had turned ashen.

"I am telling the truth, papa. She is a bad person."

"Well, let me tell you something, Julia. I don't need to live in a 10,000 square foot home to be happy. Happiness is who you are with, not where you are. And right now, being with you is the most depressing thing I can think of. You make me ashamed. Apologize to Jennifer. Do it now."

Julia looked at him sullenly.

"Julia…." Mike repeated.

"Truth, papa. Truth is what I speak."

"Damn it, Julia, you wouldn't know the truth if it hit you in the head." He paused. "What's happened to you? All you do now is think about yourself. Fine. You do that. The rest of us have a life." He rose from his chair and nodded to Jennifer. "Let's go!" he said.

Jennifer looked at Van. The older woman looked like she might faint. She went to her and placed a hand on Van's shoulder. "Van, you are a gracious hostess. You worked hard to create this wonderful dinner. I'm so very sorry the evening is ending this way."

"I'm sorry, too," Van said, anguished. She shot Julia an angry look, but Julia had retreated into herself, sitting deep in her seat with her arms folded around herself protectively.

Mike took Jennifer's hand, and together they walked out into the night.

Van watched them leave the house. Tears in her eyes, she walked back into the parlor and looked at Julia. "I hope you are happy," she said in a shaky voice. "You told me that you wanted to protect your father. Don't you understand that your behavior is going to destroy him and all the love he holds for you. Is that what you want, Julia?"

Julia stared at Van. Then she gave a self-righteous shrug, stood up and walked towards the grand staircase that led to her bedroom. *If she had to take an arrow for telling the truth, so be it. She would stand her ground.*

Chapter Twenty Two

"Class, here is your assignment," Igor intoned. One could picture the man standing at the Acropolis in the age of Aristotle, wearing a finely-woven linen Ionic purple *chiton*, the tunic that Athenian aristocrats favored. "Let yourselves go. Dream. Release yourselves. Liberate your inner mental constraints. Entrust your dreams to The Tree of Life."

The class listened, enraptured. No one had a clue as to what Igor was talking about, but the way he said it infused his words with gravitas. A few were taking notes to enable them to later probe for the deeper meaning of their mentor's pronouncements.

Igor surveyed the class, fixing his gaze on each one of them. "Now class, what I am asking lends itself to no formula. Formula reduces theatre to soap opera. We have not come here today to discover new approaches for cleaning out your head." The class laughed at his little joke. Igor gave a wry smile.

"No," Igor continued, "Our mission is to refresh the mind, to open it to the infinite possibilities that secrete the nuances of our souls. Giving expression to that is what theatre is about. We seek the specific, so that we may extract from concrete illustrations the universal truths that enable us each to make connections."

He paused theatrically and eyed Vicky. She was gripping her seat, breathless. *This Is the Igor I paid money to learn from*, she thought. Four more sentences from Igor and she'd be ready to beautify him.

"Isn't that what we have come for?" Igor continued. "Is that not, I ask, the journey upon which we embark? Is there not within each of us a desire to embark for Cythera?" Few in the class caught his reference to Jean-Antoine Watteau's painting, an allegory about the departure from Cythera, the birthplace of Venus. The painting symbolized the artist's message—happiness in the mortal world was transitory. Those who sought happiness for a lifetime did so in ignorance of the frailty of life and the brevity of its duration. Igor urged his class to embark upon their own personal journeys and give expression to their feelings.

"Wow," Vicky whispered into Linda's ear. They were seated next to each other. "Igor is *so* brilliant."

Linda nodded in agreement, then motioned Vicky to be quiet so that she could take in every syllable of what he was saying. Igor, she felt, was helping her become more in touch with herself.

Igor crossed his arms, satisfied. The class was paying close attention. He expected no less. "Let me trigger your imaginations with a story of my own. This is profoundly personal to me. I share it with few people. You will understand why. I pray it will help you reach into yourselves and then share your own story."

Julia was seated next to Jason. He whispered in her ear, "Is Igor for real? Can you make sense out of anything he's saying?"

"Shhhh!" Julia whispered back. "Pay attention. He's going to cast *Hamlet* based on how we do in this exercise. So let's see what he *really* wants."

"Yeah, yeah, okay," Jason said. Julia was correct. But Igor's flowery nonsense were not helping. Jason was sure that Igor had marked him for the role of Hamlet. Obviously only one male student fit those royal boots.

"So now, our minds wander," Igor said, beginning his story. "Once there was a woman. She was tall and beautiful. She had an aquiline face and deep green eyes that made her look as if she had risen from the depths of a great ocean. She was my teacher. I loved her. I wanted her. I could smell, taste, sense every inch of her body. That was denied to me. Instead, she offered me the power of her intellect. It radiated a mysterious force, one that drew me to her. Her gaze was proud as I knelt at her feet. She asked if I was prepared to learn. 'Yes,' I said. 'Then open your mind,' she said."

Igor paused to make certain his fable was registering. Their wide eyes and fixed stares affirmed their undivided attention. He continued. "It was through her—I shall call her Athena, for she was as wise as a Goddess—that I discovered a passion for the theatre and learned the meaning of joy and sorrow. We spent a good deal of time together. It was glorious. The days were cool and there was a breeze at our back. A warm sun beckoned us to think about heading always to the next horizon. Life is never perfect, but this was as close as we mortals are perhaps ever allowed to even approach achieving such a state."

"This is so totally awesome," Linda said under her breath to Vicky. They leaned in to hear more clearly.

Igor had paused, allowing the students a moment to process his story. His eyes lifted upward, his expression suggesting that somehow he had connected to a higher power. He continued. "But alas, as is the way with mortal life, an effort to achieve perfection begets its own obstacles. My Athena was a Goddess, it's true, but not impregnable. A rival professor saw the effect she was having on me, and on all her students. Her brilliance aroused fierce jealousy in the rival, for the rival was glib but not smart."

Igor looked at the class. "And do you know what the rival did? Listen closely class, because life is full of hidden traps. Be on the look-out for them. The rival accused Athena of seducing me."

He stopped, closed his eyes as if in pain from the long-ago

memory, then opened them and continued. "Yes, I admit that I wanted her. I was a young boy, full of love for this amazing teacher, this woman who awakened all the best in me. I wanted her more than anything on this planet." He paused and shook his head. "Ahhh, but alas, she was innocent. She had never done anything wrong. Nonetheless, the school board summoned her to answer the charges. It was her word against the rival's. Athena felt that even answering the charges lay beneath her dignity. She was entirely noble, but foolish."

He paused for a moment, then said, "The board concluded that her measured response was an admission of guilt. They fired her. Athena was wise but too sensitive—too trusting of others. Her disgrace cast a dark shadow over her existence. In an existential way she concluded that life was futile—and sad to say, not long after she was summarily dismissed, she succeeded at taking her own life. And, in passing from this world, she took a part of me with her."

Igor was on the verge of tears. That he had told this story a hundred times to different audiences did not matter. He looked at the class. "I blame myself for what happened. I wanted her. She wanted me. Universal forces joined us for larger purposes. We can each draw a lesson from the diversion of original ambition into darker channels, and the consequences that unexpectedly flow from them. So I say to you: *dream big*. Make your dreams concrete. Find the depth of emotions that motivate them, and articulate them to us from the sanctimony of the stage. In the realization of that ambition you will find true revelation about who and what you are." He paused, then bowed his head.

The class gave him a standing ovation. He looked up. "Thank you for listening to my story. Now I need each of you to write a few sentences about an incident that changed the course of your life. A single significant incident." He handed out 8 x 10 index cards and pens. You will each then place the card on a branch of that tree, which I will call the "Tree of Life." He pointed to a small potted fir tree on the side of the room—the kind of tree usually decorated with bright ornaments at Christmas. Each student scribbled something, then in turn, walked to the tree and scotch-taped their card to the tree.

Julia was sitting quietly in the corner contemplating what to put on her card. She was still thinking as Tammy, a plain, pleasantly plump woman who wore no makeup, volunteered to tell her story. She walked to Igor and stood next to him. When she spoke, she did so in a quiet voice—almost a whisper. Her life-changing story was about her boyfriend. They had lived together for several years. She loved him very much, yet he had never asked her to marry him. One day Caitlin, a former fiancé, moved back to New York from her home town in North Carolina. She contacted him, and, to Tammie's dismay, he had welcomed her back into his life.

When she protested, he admitted he had contradictory feelings. He was in love with them both. But if one of them had to go, it was Tammy. "To my embarrassment and shame," Tammy admitted, her head down, not looking at anyone, "I accepted the situation. I just didn't want to lose him. I rationalized in my head that having him to myself only half the time was better than not at all."

Igor walked over to Tammy, lifted her from her chair, and gave her a big hug. "Thank you, Tammy, for your courage. It was painful for you. Please don't beat yourself up for your very human decision."

Turning from her to the class, he said, "Sometimes, class, to have a person we love deeply remain in our lives we have to learn to share them," Igor pronounced. Julia stared at him silently, taking in his counsel.

Finally it was her turn. She was dressed in a stylish red dress and a coat with an ermine fur collar. Once on stage, she paused and cast an eye over the class. "My card is blank," she said. "I am sorry Igor. I cannot do this." Then she returned to her seat. Julia had a story, but she felt it too private to share with anyone. Silence filled the room. All eyes turned to Igor.

"Okay Julia. I respect that," he said finally, giving her a pass. "But are you willing, at some future point, to describe for us some aspect of your story—when you feel ready to trust us with it, as others have done here today?"

"I will, Igor," she promised. "I will share my story—really it's my dream—as soon as I can. I have to bring that dream into focus. For now it is too raw, too unformed."

Igor turned to the class. "You see, my friends," he intoned, "True artists have the courage to withhold the articulation of their vision until it becomes fully realized. I applaud Julia for her courage." Julia managed a weak smile. Then she gathered her things and walked passed the taunting whispers of Vicky and Linda, for once oblivious to their petty snickering. She had risen above it. A darker matter was clouding Julia's mood as she left the theatre.

Chapter Twenty Three

Colorful balloons hung from the ceilings throughout Mike's Westchester mansion. A party of sixty folks had gathered. Everyone was festively dressed, the men in dark suits, the women in cocktail dresses. A small jazz trio was playing a medley of favorites, including Mike's favorite, *New York, New York*, to which he was dancing with Jennifer. Van and Julia stood at the side of the living room chatting with Jason. Igor had broken the news to him that after graduation he would be up for a role in a new Off Broadway production—and, in the immediate future, would be playing the title role in their graduation production of *Hamlet*. Julia was overjoyed for him. Jason deserved the praise—and now success—that he was getting. She was also happy for herself, since Igor had privately advised that she would play Ophelia.

Igor's confidence in her had given her the courage to try to mend things with Jennifer and her father. Since Mike believed that love would always prevail over dark storms he was prepared to accord Julia every opportunity to accept Jennifer.

Tonight Mike was throwing this party for Jennifer, to celebrate her birthday, and to introduce her to all friends and colleagues as his serious girlfriend. Mike had also invited Jennifer's family. Her parents, an aging Ohio couple named Marny and Jack, had eagerly accepted. Jennifer had told them all about Mike, Julia, and Van. Her parents felt immense pride that Mike had fallen in love with their daughter and that Jennifer was with a distinguished business leader who held strong family values.

Told that Jennifer's parents would attend, Julia had expected a weathered steelworker or carpenter. Jack Robson turned out to be a retired orthopedic surgeon. His wife, Marny, still taught history at Ohio State University. They were warm and pleasant people with the rustic quality of native Midwesterners.

"Oooh's" and "aah's" broke out as a small band struck up the grand march from *Aida* and caterers pushed a cart bearing a huge silver almond cake with white icing and unlit candles into the room. Julia's eyes widened.

Mike stepped into the front of the band, faced his assembled guests and raised his hands, calling for silence. Someone clinked a spoon against a glass.

"Gather round everybody," Mike urged. The guests were grinning from ear to ear. They stepped forward.

"I guess you probably wondered why I gathered all of you here tonight," he ventured.

"Because we needed to be fed," joked Hank McMullen, a neighbor down the way.

Mike pointed to him. "Absolutely, Hank. In this house, we fight hunger. We do it day and night." Hank gave him the thumbs up and Mike's smile broadened.

"Actually, I have more exciting news. Tonight, my friends—my dear great friends and wonderful family—two distinguished individuals have blessed us with their presence." Mike walked over to Jennifer's parents and put his arm around her father's and mother's shoulders. "They have come a long way to join us. We honor them. They are terrific people. They have also produced a special daughter, Jennifer Robson. Tonight, Jennifer" —he smiled at Jennifer and she returned it with a smile that could have lit up a thousand candles— "is celebrating her 42nd birthday."

One of the caterer's staff had lit the candles, and Mike beckoned

Jennifer forward with an outstretched hand. "Jennifer, please come up here and blow out the candles on your cake. And I hope you're not mad at me, darling, for mentioning which birthday it is. Am I in trouble?"

Her grin was wider than the Hudson River. "Mike, you are so thoughtful and such a dear. This is a lovely surprise." Jennifer blew out the candles and made a wish. She looked at Mike. "And thank you for flying mom and dad in to share this moment with us."

Mike asked Jennifer's parents to join him and their daughter. The Robsons stepped forward. Marny Robson responded for the couple, proclaiming their pride in their daughter and thanking Mike for his hospitality.

"We hope you'll come visit us real soon," Marny said. "Just be sure the word Buckeye lifts your heart." The mention of Ohio State's mascot prompted wide grins.

"Thank you, Marny." Mike took stock. His eyes danced. "Well, for those of you who like cake, this cake came from Le Dueurx." Everyone applauded. They knew that was the finest baker in Manhattan. Mike lifted the knife, ready to cut a slice. "I promise you're going to relish every bite." Everyone laughed. "However, you're going to have to wait." He looked at Jennifer, then at his guests.

"First, I'd like to say a few words." He looked for Julia, and he spotted her staring at him from behind one of the columns in their livingroom. She was standing beside a framed black-and-white photograph of herself and PH. He hesitated, but his daughter's bizarre attitude did not halt him.

Mike said: "As all of you know, life has blessed me. It blessed me with my first wife, one of the most amazing human beings God has ever put on this planet. I miss her every day of my life. I'm thankful for the time we were given to spend together and the time that we spent with our daughter, Julia." People applauded, looking around for Julia, who was still hiding behind the pillar. At the mention of Julia's name Jennifer applauded the loudest, with a broad smile.

Mike turned back to the guests. "I've also been blessed with success professionally. Adding to my blessings has been the company of Van, the mother of my late wife and grandmother to my beautiful daughter Julia." There was more applause. Van took a slight bow.

Suddenly Mike walked over to the pillar where Julia was hiding, and gently pulled her out, guiding her to the front of the room as he stepped over to Jennifer and took her hand in his free hand. As he continued to hold onto Julia, he continued: "As I said, most of all I've been blessed by the most remarkable—and yes, challenging" —some knowing laughter broke out as he grinned— "young lady named Julia. She has been the apple of my eye. She always will be." He leaned over and kissed Julia on the cheek. Julia beamed at the unexpected attention.

"Thank you, papa," she said. *Where was this all leading?* she wondered. *What was he working up to?*

Mike dropped both hands he was holding and addressed the gathering. "If there is one thing each of us has learned about life, it's that we move forward. No matter how much we achieve in life, life beckons, as if to say *show us more*. We have to keep moving. We have to be bold. I am cheered to report that my life is moving forward. In a way it is a starting over. And I have one person to thank for this incredible and wonderful change in my life." He looked directly at Jennifer. He took her hand, smiled and said, softly, "You, Jennifer. *You* have changed my life."

Tears were streaming down Jennifer's face. Her body was quivering. She covered her mouth with her hands, sensing where Mike was headed. "I have one more thing to say," he said. Mike dropped to his knees. Tears of joy streamed down Jennifer's cheeks as Mike looked straight into her eyes. "Jennifer Robson," he said solemnly, "will you please do me the honor of becoming my wife? Will you marry me?"

Jennifer was crying as she beckoned Mike to rise. When he was standing right in front of her she gave him a shaky smile and said out loud, "Yes. Yes, Mike. I would be honored to marry you." She threw her arms around him and they kissed deeply. One could have heard a pin drop as the drama unfolded. Mike reached into his pocket and took out a blue velvet case from Cartier and presented it to Jennifer, who slowly opened it. Inside, sparkling majestically in the light, was a perfect five-carat emerald-cut diamond engagement ring set in platinum, it's beauty enhanced by two slender diamond baguettes. Jennifer removed the ring and held it up for everyone to behold. Except for Julia, everyone erupted in cheers and well-wishes. Their enthusiasm and energy seemed to shake the house on its foundations.

Jennifer stared at her ring. Mike's gift was spectacular. His adoring expression dazzled her as he slipped the ring onto her left ring finger. Then he drew her to him, and with the flourish of Fred Astaire, leaned her over backwards, and theatrically kissed her again. His obvious love for his new fiancé made the moment magical.

Julia watched the unfolding proposal with ill-concealed horror. She turned and ran up the staircase to her room, first grabbing a bottle of liquor from the bar. Entering, she fixed on her mother's wedding dress, draped around a mannequin. She slammed the door shut and sat on the floor, huddled in a corner, sobbing tears of anger and betrayal as she took swallows from the bottle. She crawled to the dress. Delicately caressing the lace hem, she looked up at it and rose to her feet. Without hesitation she unzipped the dress, took it off the mannequin and put it on.

In her tipsy state, she began to dance around the room, twirling the train of the dress behind her. She remembered that her mother's veil sat in a hat box in her walk-in closet. She went and got it. She stepped into a pair of delicate white heels and went to a full length mirror to admire herself.

Outside her bedroom window, she heard the sounds of cars and people and snuck a peek out the window from behind her thick drapes. She looked down at the front entrance and saw her father and Jennifer saying their goodbyes to all the guests. Van had turned back inside. Julia pretended it was she herself on Mike's arm, not Jennifer.

Finally it was just Mike and Jennifer standing in the doorway. Julia took another sip from the liquor bottle. Jennifer and Mike lingered, kissing hungrily on the steps. Then she got into Mike's car. His driver Max was at the wheel and the car left.

Julia closed her eyes and remembered how Igor had advised her to let her dreams flow freely. He said that only then could she find the truth and security of her own identity. To follow his suggestion and to try to calm her agitated state she let her mind wander. She slowly inhaled and exhaled, entering a hypnotic state. Time seemed to stand still in her inebriated state of hazy confusion and pain.

Images floated passed her. It was nighttime. She was a young girl again, clad in an embroidered silk nightgown. In her fantasy, the sounds of her parent's love-making wafted through, and she padded down the hall and silently observed her parent's communion. But this time, everything changed: her mother looked up from beneath her husband's body and cackled at Julia, mocking her. Then she saw that it was not her mother giving forth the evil laugh. The figure under Mike's body morphed from her mother's face to her own. It glared demonically at her. Then it changed once again, and now

172

Jennifer's face was moaning in ecstasy beneath her father's body.

Julia recoiled. The vision blurred. She found herself turning round and round in a circle, unable to stop. Fear and passion ravaged her body as she became dizzy and the room swirled around her. Confused as to what was real and what was a dream, she looked in the mirror and saw PH dressed in the beautiful wedding gown. Finally, she and her mother were one and the same. Julia had assumed her mother's identity, convincing herself that Mike was her husband and that she needed to rescue him from Jennifer.

Her dream shifted. Now she was stumbling in the hallway. It was dark, silent, and hauntingly empty. The image of Jennifer wearing a short silk nightgown materialized. Jennifer was smiling like a victorious warrior who has vanquished her fiercest enemy. As Julia stared at her nemesis, a large steel knife with jagged edges appeared in Julia's hands and she launched herself at her father's new fiancé, stabbing Jennifer repeatedly. Blood spurted from Jennifer's face and body.

Jennifer raised her arms defensively, screaming and begging for her life. Julia kept cutting and slicing. Finally Jennifer lay silent, her body still, he life's blood running out onto a cold marble floor.

Julia woke from her nightmare with a piercing scream.

Chapter Twenty Four

The bar, Joe's, was a typical New York take on a small town pub. It was brick with grey walls and a large, green-felt covered pool table. A half dozen blue collar workers in plaid shirts and jeans were gathered around it, shooting pool, drinking beer and exchanging dirty jokes. They were patriotic working stiffs, men up at 6:00 a.m. and hard at it until the 4:30 whistle blew. Then it was Miller Time. They had gathered at their local watering hole, where the beer was cold and the bourbon cheap.

Plastic covered booths lined both walls. All the booths were occupied by couples or small groups of friends. Several men, workers on a nearby construction site two blocks away, sat on barstools at one end of the bar, drinking and tossing down handfuls of salty pretzels and peanuts. At the end of the long polished maple bar sat Julia, a drink in front of her, angry, confused, and broken-hearted. She was the one who belonged in Mike's life. Mike's marriage proposal to Jennifer had turned Julia's world upside down. Then her nightmare pushed her over the edge. *How can this be happening?* She asked herself the question over and over. *None of the answers made any sense. What about her? Where would she fit into Mike's life? Was he planning to cast her adrift? Why could he not love her romantically?* Reality had blurred.

Jennifer had won. That was all she could think of. That terrible greedy woman had tricked her father into giving her a ring. First, a ring on her hand, next, a collar around his neck. She imagined Jennifer immersing herself in Mike's business and then cutting him off from those he loved. She had heard of this before: new wives that

175

wanted nothing to do with the husband's old life—not with friends, not with family, and especially not with daughters.

Jennifer! Gold digger! The words ran through Julia's mind as she downed her first drink and ordered another rum-sour cocktail. The bartender, an obese man with a thick mustache and wrinkled skin, served her a second round. She gulped it down. She felt flummoxed. Jennifer had tricked Mike and out-foxed her.

She cringed at the implications. She had a consuming love for Mike. He was the rock that provided a foundation for her existence. She struggled with her sense of self, separate from her mother's. She could no longer deny her obsession. She loved her father not only as a daughter. She wanted him in bed, making love to her as he had to her mother.

The bartender reluctantly served up a third drink to the obviously drunk Julia, who again gulped it down. The alcohol had gotten to her. Constraints fell away. A plain vision emerged. Julia knew what needed to be done. Jennifer had to go—voluntarily or involuntarily.

Julia ordered a fourth rum-sour. The bartender resisted. She barked at him, "I'm fine, just bring me another drink!" She took a $100 bill out of her purse and laid it on the bar. The bartender eyed her, took the cash and made her the drink, although he kept the alcohol to a minimum. Still, to Julia, a young woman who seldom drank, the Meyers dark rum tasted rich and robust.

Optimism surging, Julia made a plan. Her father might marry the fraudster. But she was going to give it her best shot to make him see the truth. Let the world laugh. Her father belonged to her, not Jennifer. *She, not Jennifer, cared about her father.*

At first she ignored the sounds coming from the television which was mounted high on the wall behind the bar. Then something penetrated her foggy brain and caused her to look up. She noticed that something called *The Drew Pinsky Show* was on. Best known as "Dr. Drew," the celebrity doctor, who was board-certified in internal medicine, had become an addiction specialist. What caught Julia's ear was the particular "addiction" this episode centered on. The "scroll" —the copy that appeared on the bottom of the screen—said "Genetic Sexual Attraction is a Growing Phenomenon." Dr. Drew was talking about a pregnant and troubled young woman who was on his show seeking advice on what to do about her tragic situation.

Julia asked the bartender to turn up the volume. He obliged. Julia leaned in to hear the conversation. Dr. Drew's guest fascinated her. Women got pregnant every day, but *this* woman was pregnant by her own father. Julia knew that incest was a criminal act. Why was this woman brave enough, or perhaps foolish enough, to go public?

Julia listened intently as Dr. Drew explained that the term Genetic Sexual Attraction, or GSA for short, was first coined in the U.S. in the late 1980s by Barbara Gonyo, the founder of "Truth Seekers In Adoption," a Chicago-based support group for adoptees and their new-found relatives. The emergence of GSA, both in the US and the UK, coincided with the relaxation of adoption laws in the mid-1970s, which gave adopted children easier access to their records. This in turn led to an increase in the number of reunions between adoptees and their blood relatives. Today, Dr. Drew reported, GSA was on the rise. The increase in fertility options and new technologies made it easier for people to track down their long-lost genetic parent, child, sibling or other relative.

It raised the taboo subject of incest that no-one wanted to talk about. But GSA is real, Dr. Drew noted, and the condition affects 1 in 500 families. Julia was startled. That could add up to a great number of people who meet their biological relative in adulthood, then fall romantically in love with them.

After finishing his preliminary explanation, Dr. Drew brought out that guest, "Amy." Amy was distraught. Drew took pains to reassure her. The specifics of this young woman's situation were heartbreaking. Her parents had divorced when she was only three. Her father had abandoned the family and moved to another city. By accident—having no idea that they were related—she and her father met. She was twenty-three at the time—Julia's age. Unexpectedly, and purely by accident, she had met her father, and was blissfully ignorant of the fact that the handsome older man she had fallen in love with was her own father.

Julia watched, transfixed, as the woman related emotions and feelings that seemed to echo her own deeply-felt sentiments. "Amy," Dr. Drew said in a kind voice, "Genetic Sexual Attraction is a recognized syndrome. You fell in love with a stranger. You didn't know he was your father. That means you have nothing to feel guilty about. I am not minimizing your dilemma, of course, but now that you know—and with a child on the way—you have some serious issues to resolve."

The guys at the end of the bar had been watching the show. The one nearest to Julia, a heavily tattooed and muscular man with thick lips and biceps that looked like they could lift a tank, scowled. "Those sick fuckers," he barked down the length of the bar. "Doesn't anybody have any sense of decency anymore?" "You tell 'em," one of his co-workers nodded. He was a thin, wiry man with stubble covering his face. "I don't get it. Why is this poor excuse for a doctor coddling these perverts on the tube? I say send them to the slammer or put 'em out of their misery altogether!"

The others nodded and clinked beer bottles in agreement. Julia's eyes fluctuated between the workers making those harsh judgments and *The Doctor Drew Show*. She picked up the cocktail glass in front of her and downed the remainder of her fourth rum-sour. *I always knew who my father was, so maybe I don't have that exact thing,* she told herself, not remembering the name of the condition. Still, she had to admit the hard reality: that she was sexually attracted to her father. She felt sick. *What does that make me,* she wondered, her thoughts feverish. *Was she a monster? Did she belong on a television show, being interviewed about her incestuous feelings for the titillation of the masses? Would they have even more fun mocking her terrible accent and bi-racial confusion? Oh if only the floor could open up and swallow her whole!*

Horrified, confused, and dizzy, Julia clambered off her stool and staggered outside. The bouncer at the door cast a sideways look at her. Drunk, Julia looked around helplessly. The bouncer realized she was completely out of it and kept an eye on her as she teetered on her heels and moved a little ways down the sidewalk.

Julia could hardly see straight. Her vision was blurred and her balance was off. After fifty paces, she braced herself against a red Fiat and tried to stand upright. Facing her in a store window was a mannequin in a white wedding gown. Delirious, she imagined the woman in the gown was Jennifer. She saw Jennifer's face, mocking her as she had in the dream, her features maliciously contorted. The intensity of the imagined laughter reached a fever pitch. Finding a brick on the curb, Julia picked it up and hurled it at the mannequin.

The brick shattered the plate glass window and set off a burglar alarm. Julia grimaced as her stomach turned inside out. She threw up on the sidewalk, then fell to the ground. The bouncer pulled out his cell phone and dialed 911. Then he ran over to Julia. Minutes later, the sound of sirens cut through the air.

"Take it easy," the bouncer said. He tried to gently raise her up off the sidewalk. "Help's on the way."

Julia turned her face up to him. The bouncer gulped. Beneath the blood that trickled from a small cut in her forehead, tears soaked her face.

Chapter Twenty Five

The phone call to Mike had come as a relief. After Julia had run out of their house in the middle of the night, he, Jennifer, and Van had been frantically calling Julia's friends but no one had seen her. Mike wasn't sure whether to be angry or frightened. Actually, he was both.

Any adult would punish a youngster for acting out as Julia had done. Her disappearance from the party had upset him as well as Van. Asian families profoundly respect grandmothers. And, as Mike realized, despite Van's vigorous spirits, she was slowing down. A shock to her emotions such as Julia had inflicted lately had to threaten Van's well-being. This was the last straw. Still, he wouldn't stop worrying until he made certain Julia was safe. Jennifer showed equal concern. She knew that a daughter who hated her father's fiancé and future wife could tear apart the most tightly-knit relationships.

The caller was Captain Otis Johnson of the 83rd precinct police station. Happily, after receiving emergency medical attention for a cut, a few bruises and a pervasive hangover, EMS personnel had pronounced her ready to be released. Still, she had committed a public act of drunken behavior and vandalism. There was a stiff fine to be paid, or she might be facing a criminal record, or even jail time.

Mike's car was right outside and he and Jennifer jumped in. They rushed to the police station. Knowing how Julia felt about his fiancé, Mike cautioned that they had to tread carefully. No one could predict what kind of emotional state they would find her in.

Arriving at the police precinct, they agreed that the better judgment was for Jennifer to wait in the car while he went inside to settle matters. Captain Johnson proved to be a no-nonsense street cop. He recognized that Julia's erratic behavior was an exception to her normal conduct. Johnson let Mike use the phone in his office and Mike contacted the store owner. He apologized profusely for his daughter and promised to make good on any costs or business losses by noon the next day.

Fortunately the owner was an elderly man who understood. As he put it, "Those dang millennials just can't keep it together, can they? At least we oldies know how to hold our liquor without shattering glass!" Mike vigorously concurred. Twenty minutes of courteous conversation with the store owner and payment of the police's stiff fine put this latest crisis behind the Chamonix family.

A moment later Julia appeared, escorted by a female police officer. Her forehead bore a small bandage from the flying glass her hurled brick had shattered. Her dazed face and wrinkled clothing revealed everything. She and Mike looked at one another silently. Then Mike went to his daughter and held her tightly. "Princess, I was so worried. It's going to be all right. I'm here."

Julia managed a thin smile. "Hi, father."

He kissed her on the forehead. She burrowed into his arms, as he explained that he had spoken with the shop owner, and that when Mike agreed to immediately call a repair company and pay for the broken front window, also explaining that his daughter was under some terrible stress lately and had never done anything like this before, he had agreed to drop all charges.

Clearly Mike still loved her, Julia thought, or he would not have come to her rescue, with thankfully no Jennifer in sight! Maybe this was the turning point she and father needed. He had worried about her, and now here he was. Things were looking up.

"Let's go home. Car's outside. Why don't you get in and wait for me while I sign some papers so we can make this thing go away?" Julia nodded and walked outside slowly, weak from her ordeal.

After she walked out, a thought occurred to Mike. Julia had committed what the police *could* have characterized as a serious offense. He had read the police report. She had been less than cooperative when the EMS team arrived, followed by a police unit. Only the pleading of the EMS people, supported by the bar's bouncer, had persuaded the police to refrain from placing her under formal arrest. They had radioed the station for instructions. Captain Johnson had taken the call, and gave Julia a break after realizing who her father was. Leniency in these tense times, when police felt under assault from all quarters, was a welcome gesture.

Mike looked at Johnson. "Captain Johnson, I want you to know that *I* know you've gone beyond the call of duty for Julia. Our business is done here so I don't see any ethical issues, but," he drew a breath, "what if I sent over two tickets to Julia's graduation play? It's Shakespeare. She has a lead. Don't know if you enjoy Shakespeare...." his voice trailed off.

"My wife and I both do," the police captain said enthusiastically. "Well, sir, you don't have to do that, but actually we would be honored to watch your daughter perform."

"Perfect!" Mike reached inside his coat pocket for a small notebook and his gold Monte Blanc pen and scribbled a note to himself. The officer and his wife would enjoy front row seats next to Jennifer, Van, and himself. "Consider it done."

As that conversation unfolded, Julia was walking out to the car. She felt shaky. She had been inebriated and in a highly charged emotional state. She vaguely remembered seeing some program on television that had upset her, and then the sound of glass shattering. She had overheard a discussion between Captain Johnson and the two officers on the beat who had answered the call. Julia understood a new kind of fear. She aspired to be a performer, a public figure. People would scrutinize her past, present, and future. Would a criminal record burden her future?

Her father had saved the day. *Her father had rescued her.* She spied Mike's car in the parking lot. Julia reached for the handle to open the side passenger door to sit next to Mike when he returned. Abruptly she realized that Jennifer was seated in the back. Julia's eyes widened as Jennifer rolled down the right side's back window, stuck her head out, and smiled. Julia froze, speechless.

She turned and ran off down the street, ignoring traffic.

"Julia, wait!" Jennifer cried out. She jumped out of the car and charged after Julia. "Please, stop. I want to talk," she shouted. Julia only ran faster. Jennifer picked up speed, hoping to catch the young girl and talk sense into her. "Julia! Stop! Please, don't do this!"

Julia was running unevenly. Jennifer afraid that Julia might stumble and hit her head on the sidewalk, was running after her, trying to catch up. Behind her, Jennifer heard a shout. Glancing over her shoulder she saw Mike, on the steps of the precinct, taking in the chaotic scene.

Neither women saw the approaching sedan bearing down on them. The driver slammed on his brakes. Julia managed to leap out of the way. Jennifer was less fortunate. The vehicle smashed into Jennifer, knocking her backwards. On the street she lay quietly, unmoving, as Mike ran up to her, calling out for help.

Julia stumbled over to where her father sat beside Jennifer. He was gently cradling her bleeding head as she lay unconscious in the middle of the street.

Chapter Twenty Six

Jennifer was lying in a luxurious hospital room in the Special Patient wing of Columbia Presbyterian. Part of the hospital's unique concierge wing, it could have doubled for a large room at the Ritz-Carlton. A bandage covered the cut on her forehead. A leading plastic surgeon had closed the wound with five stitches and swore it would leave only the faintest of scars.

Mike treated his fiancé like royalty. He had filled the room with fragrant lilies, a few dozen roses, and other flowers. He had also brought her some delicious non-hospital food. Seated in a plush chair next to Jennifer's bed, he held her hand, waiting for her to wake up.

Julia stood silently in the corner, the hangover from last night's alcohol-fueled debacle giving her a massive headache. Exhausted, wanting nothing more than to be invisible, she watched her father as he sat beside Jennifer's bed and held her hand. Jealous of his tenderness towards the woman, she wondered how soon she could legitimately leave the hospital and go lie down at home. But no, Jennifer had begun to stir.

"Hi, sweetheart," Mike said to Jennifer as she awakened. He kissed her hand.

"Hi, you," Jennifer smiled. Abruptly she became aware of her extravagant surroundings. "Is this heaven?" she remarked quietly, looking around at the sumptuous hospital suite usually reserved for celebrities. "I've never seen a hospital room like this."

"The concierge service at Columbia Presbyterian," Mike smiled.

"Wow," Jennifer whispered, lifting his hand to her lips and giving it a return kiss. Thank you for taking care of me."

Mike cocked his head. "Hey, you don't expect your fiancé to provide less than the best for his sweetheart, do you?"

"Of course not," Jennifer said with a grin. Looking around, she became aware of Julia in the corner of the room, inching towards the door. Jennifer was gracious. "Hello, Julia." she said evenly. "How are you doing?"

Julia remained mute. Mike looked at Julia with a hard expression. "Julia, Jennifer is being gracious, but you owe her a very strong apology. She was running after you. If you had acted like an adult and gotten in the car to wait for me none of this would have happened."

Julia took in her father's words and harsh tone, but remained silent. Angrier yet at her stubborn refusal to take responsibility for her behavior, Mike continued his severe criticism. "And even beyond an apology, Julia, you need to change your attitude. I don't know what your reasons may be for why you have acted as you have ever since Jennifer came into our lives, but there is no excuse! You have said you would change your behavior before, and then worse things have happened, this being the last straw! This nonsense ends here and now. We're all going to be family together—a happy family."

He looked at his daughter intently. "Agreed?"

Julia was trapped. There was no way out. She walked over to the hospital bed and looked down mutely. In spite of everything, she still couldn't force herself to apologize. Most of all what she was sorry for was that her father had ever met this woman. But that was one regret she would keep to herself.

"No worries," Jennifer filled the awkward silence. Then she looked up at Mike. "Have you spoken to the doctors? Am I going to live?"

"Are you going to live?" Mike repeated theatrically. "Let me tell you something, Mrs. Wife-to-be. You will not only live, you will be better than ever when you leave here, because we have a great big lavish wedding to plan."

Jennifer's eyes widened. "I can do that. I know it'll be hard, but you can trust me. I'll give it the ole' college try." She and Mike laughed.

Jennifer turned to look up at Julia. "Julia, I hope you're going to help us plan this wedding. I wouldn't think of doing it without you."

Julia gave Jennifer a small smile, but didn't respond. She had no interest in planning this woman's wedding to her father.

Dr. Anderson, the attending physician, entered the room. He was holding Jennifer's patient file. A nurse accompanied him. Mike stood up and shook his hand.

"So," Mike wondered, "how's our patient? Will she be able to leave soon? That is, if she wants to. This suite is pretty nice!"

Dr. Anderson was a tall man with high cheekbones and closely cropped hair. He wore golden wirerim glasses. His expression had a natural warmth that was reflected in his intelligent eyes. He eyed his patient. "Mrs." —he looked at Mike—" or is it Ms. Robson?"

"We're getting married, but right now it's Ms. Robson," Mike said.

Mike looked at Dr. Anderson. "Well, what's the prognosis?"

The doctor's expression turned serious. "First and most important," he answered, fixing his eyes on Jennifer, "you will recover quickly. You'll need to stay here for another day, and then we can release you. Your blood tests are all normal. We did a CT scan. There was no internal bleeding inside your head, even though you did hit the pavement hard. Lucky woman!" He paused. "Aside from the scratches on your forehead, you suffered a minor concussion and

187

your shoulder blades have bone bruises. These should resolve themselves over the next day or two, at home."

Mike was thrilled and squeezed Jennifer's hand. The relief on his face required no elaboration. Julia was smiling as well, reassured that her flight hadn't caused any disastrous long-term consequences.

Dr. Anderson took a longer pause. He rechecked his notes. He fixed them with a solemn expression. "I do have one unhappy piece of news. I am sorry to bear sad tidings. But my responsibility as your physician is to tell you the truth."

Mike's body tightened. Dr. Anderson looked at Jennifer. "I am sorry, but we were not able to save the baby."

Mike's jaw dropped. Julia's face twisted. They both eyed Jennifer. Jennifer returned their stares. She spoke nervously, in halting tones. "Mike, I was going to tell you. I just found out myself. Then all of this happened. There was no time."

Mike looked for his daughter, but she was no longer in the room. Unable to bear her shock at learning that Jennifer had been carrying her father's child—the baby that, due to the accident, she had now miscarried—Julia had fled.

Chapter Twenty Seven

A distraught Mike sat across the coffee table from Van, his face drawn. He was wearing a plaid shirt, khaki pants and a light yellow Merino wool sweater. Van was wearing a black smock, as if she was in mourning, which is how she felt. Two days had elapsed since the hospital had released Jennifer, who was now resting at home with the nurse Mike had sent to help her recover. After Dr. Anderson had broken the shocking news that Jennifer had been pregnant and lost the baby, a shadow had descended upon Mike's household.

The news had shaken even Van. Mike had spent the day at home, making certain that the jolt didn't produce a catastrophic impact on Van and her increasingly fragile health.

"Mike, what does Julia say?" Van asked, with tired eyes.

"Nothing. She won't talk. She's frozen up on me." His face was rigidly glum.

Van shook her head. "Jennifer had an obligation to tell you," Van said. "But I believe that, as she told you, she has just found out she was pregnant, and had no time to tell you before we got that call about Julia and you had to go right over to the police station."

"Julia thinks Jennifer was playing me all along, and deliberately got pregnant," Mike said, not believing it, but needing to confide in Van.

Van was deeply troubled by all of this. "Mike, your daughter, my granddaughter, is a darling young woman. We both love her. We also both know that she indulges herself in fantasies. What's happened tells me that these may have grown destructive."

"Well, this sure as hell makes things more difficult. Julia will

189

be more than ever convinced that the only thing Jennifer's after is my bank account," Mike said morosely. "The truth is, if Jennifer genuinely loves me, she's welcome to everything I have, and more. I gave her my heart, and that includes sharing my worldly goods. Thankfully, there's plenty for everyone." He paused and added, "Neither you nor Julia will ever be homeless or go hungry."

"That doesn't need to be said, Mike. You have always been a good and generous provider. We both know it," Van replied.

Mike had been so pre-occupied with the news of a lost baby that he had not paid close attention to Julia's whereabouts. He tapped his hand on the counter. "Where *is* Julia now? Is she here?"

"No. She comes and goes but has said nothing. She was here last night, but she left early this morning with her books. Probably she is in class."

Mike suspected his daughter was avoiding him. But his priority was to clear the air with Jennifer. Later that day, he sat beside Jennifer on her couch and listened to her explanation.

"Mike, I was just waiting for the right time." She looked at him helplessly. "I'm so sorry, Mike. Sorry we lost the baby. This was such an unbelievably fantastic thing—the idea of bearing you a child at age 42. I was in heaven after I took a pregnancy test—in fact I took a few just to be sure—and they were all positive. You have no idea how excited I was. I spent hours planning how I was going to tell you."

She started to say more, but her sobs took over. Her words and body language moved Mike to tears. He gently put his arms around her. "It's all right, my love. It's all right. Everything's going to be wonderful. I understand." He gazed directly into her eyes. "Jennifer, I love you. I'm going to marry you. We will have a child, and that child will grow up as we grow old and make us proud. I can't imagine life without you. We're going to make our lives together."

"Grow old and have gray hair together?" she laughed.

He shook his head vigorously. "*I* may go gray. But in my eyes, you will stay young and fresh forever. No matter how many birthdays we celebrate, every year we're going to grow younger at heart." He kissed her chin. "All thanks to you."

"Mike, I love you so much," she cried, and broke into tears. She threw her arms around him.

"I love you, too, kiddo. Now and forever," Mike assured her.

Chapter Twenty Eight

The Honduran Coffee & Bakery Shop was located on East 73rd Street just off Lexington Avenue. A small but intimate place, it had a dozen wooden tables, racks of magazines and newspapers, and big jars of coffee beans from all parts of the world on display for customers. The counter featured an assortment of banana bread, carrot cake, and blueberry muffins. Mozart and Bach provided a chic resonance for the Upper East Side elite. Julia was serving a latte to a customer as Jason and Van entered. Julia had trouble meeting her grandmother's eyes.

"Hey Julia. Everyone's looking for you," Jason said. "Your father went to acting class to try and find you. Bethany told him you were staying with her. He knows you don't want to see him. Van and I decided we'd come see you ourselves."

Julia came from behind the counter and kissed Van on the cheek. "Hello grandmother," she said. Her manner was subdued.

"Julia, your father and I are very worried. Are you all right?"

"Of course, grandma." She cast an eye at Bethany, who also worked at the shop. "Bethany, can you cover for me?"

Bethany nodded, happy to help. "Take a table. I'll bring over some tea and muffins."

"Thanks Bethany," Van said. She had met Julia's friend at the costume party. She remembered names. While Jason ordered an espresso at the counter, Van and Julia settled in at a back table. Van wasted no time. She told Julia, "Your father misses you. We all do."

"I understand, grandma. I just needed time to think things through."

"Good, Julia. I'm happy to hear that. Well, I'm not fine."

Julia winced. She saw that Van was looking unwell and felt guilty. "I'm sorry. I didn't mean to hurt you. I have been confused." Her voice trailed off. Bethany delivered two steaming cups of fragrant tea.

Van spoke in a harsh tone, which took Julia aback. Even when angry, she had never raised her voice to Julia. "Look at how skinny you are. What are you trying to do? Punish your body?" She shook her head. Julia stared at her numbly. Van continued. "Thanks to you—*you, Julia, and your selfishness*—you may have ruined your relationship with your father. You have also put a cloud over his relationship with Jennifer, which is unfair." She raised her voice. "You have no right. You are not the only person in this world. The rest of us have feelings too."

Each word cracked like a whip. Julia eyed her tearfully. Her expression paled.

Van wasn't through. "When are you going to talk to him?"

"Papa does not want me," Julia responded plaintively. "He used to love me. Now he has Jennifer. He saves all his love for the social climber."

"You sound like a twelve-year old," Van snapped. "Julia, you're better than this."

"This is all papa's fault."

"Look, I did not come here to point fingers. I came to talk sense into you," Van lectured. "I do not know what will happen between your father and Jennifer. He has told Jennifer they need to take a break. Now he is all alone—just like me. She paused. "Ever since your mother died all I have is you. I helped raise you. I made sure, along with your father, that you were clothed and fed. I had your clothes washed and ironed. I helped you study. You grew up as my

194

granddaughter. You made me proud. Now, I'm not so sure."

Julia was crying. Van waved aside her tears. "Stop crying and listen to me. Your life means everything to me. I can't stand seeing you like this."

"What do you want me to do?" Julia cried.

"Find your father. He needs you. You need him." She shook her head, fed up. In her mind, she was giving Julia one more chance. "You are expected home for dinner. If we do not see you, pack your belongings and leave us. Your leaving will cause us much sorrow, but the choice is yours. We have reached the end of our tolerance. Behave like an adult or be gone."

Jason walked over to see if they needed anything. Van gave him a reassuring pat on the arm. "Jason, you are good young man. Perhaps she will listen to you. She thinks she has a bad life. Wait until she meets the real world."

Van stood up and without a further word, walked out of the coffee shop.

Julia recognized that this was a debacle. She looked at Jason. "I guess I've really done it, haven't I?"

He clasped Julia's arm. "Make it right, Julia. I know you can."

"This is hard."

"Welcome to the real world."

Julia smiled weakly. "What should I do?"

"What Van said. It's decision time. You've got to decide what matters in your life. You're the only one who can make that choice. But you're out of time."

She took in his advice and nodded slowly. Attempting to lighten the mood, he changed topics. "Hey, Igor wants us at full dress rehearsal this week." He became excited. "Casting directors, producers, agents—they're all coming to see the final production. This is our opportunity for a big break. But you've got to get it together."

His words had a discernible impact. Julia furrowed her eyebrows and nodded agreement. Jason continued, "Everyone loves a winner. They like it even better when *everybody wins*. Come on, Julia. We've got lots to do, and we're going to do it together. Put a vision in your head. A vision of success—and a vision of your family watching you achieve that success. Can you do that?" He gave her a penetrating look.

The color returned to her face. She leaned over and touched Jason's arm. "Thank you, Jason. Grandma is right to like you so much. I think I do too."

"Doing Ophelia is going to require your full concentration." Jason said. "You can't let other emotions distract you." He paused. "Your families your concern. But we're a team. Babe, I need you with me. I need you to get your mind in the game."

Julia took Jason's point. He was kind, he had a big heart, he liked her, he respected her. He gave her good advice. The task before them was the production. She resolved not to let Jason down.

"I'm there for you, Jason," she declared. "Count me in."

He gave her his brightest smile, and a thumbs up. "Right on, Julia. We're knocking this one out of the ballpark. Best of all, you won't let *yourself* down. "

"You're the best, Jason," Julia exclaimed

His grin broadened. "Right. Don't you forget it."

Chapter Twenty Nine

A Terrible Loss

Grandma was at home, kneeling on a cushion as she prayed over the little Buddhist altar she had set up in her own house, the modest one she had bought for herself when she first landed in the US. Although living with Mike and Julia, she retained possession of her house and kept it as her humble retreat. Once in a while, when she felt she needed alone time to nurture and heal her own soul, she went there for solitude and peace.

Now she was praying for Julia's soul, asking the spiritual deities to grant forgiveness, mercy, and understanding to her granddaughter, the person she cherished most in the world.

"That young woman is still an innocent child," Van prayed. "She has a good heart. Heavenly deities, please inspire her to do right, not only for herself, but for her father, for Jennifer, for friends, and for all those around her, who deeply care about her."

The encounter with Julia at the coffee shop had left Van distraught. Julia was such an interesting, talented, and unique person. She had a way of inspiring others. But now there was a certain seed that had sown in her mind, making her act in weird and cruel ways. Van could not understand what had gotten into her beloved granddaughter to make her act so out of character.

Suddenly, the silver-framed crayon drawing of her family, all four of them, happy and smiling, that Julia had drawn as a child, fell over, glass shattering, the sound reverberating. At the same moment Van felt a sharp pain in her chest, as if someone had thrust a knife into her fragile rib cage. Grabbing her cane to steady herself, Van tried to regain her balance, but fell to the floor, all in one fluid motion, like a branch falling from a tree in a sudden wind. Her body jerked. Lying on the floor, she clutched her chest, then, mercifully the pain ended. She died immediately.

****

Julia was distraught. She and everyone who knew and loved Van wanted her precious life to go on forever, like million-year mountains and seas. Now she was gone. Nonetheless, Julia sensed Van's soul nearby. It was invisible, formless, and belonged to a different world, but Julia could intuitively felt that she was present. She knew that Van was in Nirvana, looking back to the Earth, pityingly gazing down at her grandchild, but not condemning her. Knowing Van, her selflessness, she might even feel deep regret for somehow failing Julia on behalf of her deceased mother. But Julia knew it was she who had failed Van.

After the burial, there had been a small catered reception in Van's own home—the house where she died from a heart attack. Everyone appeared in dark clothing. The atmosphere was gloomy. In fact, the whole world seemed gloomier. Van's death had left an enotional emptiness in those that knew her, whether they knew her well or slightly. In her quiet way, she had been a major influence on so many people, friends, and strangers.

Jennifer had attended the reception, and hesitantly asked Mike about his after-the-reception plans. He told her that he wanted to stay in the house alone a little more, so he could think about Van's life and the many lessons she had taught him. Mike had always respected Van, from their very first meeting in Vietnam. He was thankful to the spiritual deities who had bestowed their blessings on him by allowing Van to remain in his life after Phuong Ha died.

He and Julia had not seen each other since the engagement party and he had hoped she would stay in the house with him. That way he could try to break their emotional estrangement. He believed Van's death would turn things around.

Across the livingroom, Mike watched as Julia walked around quietly, seeming to be in a daze as she lightly touched her grandmother's possessions, clearly lamenting the loss of her grandmother. The Hermes scarf that she had tied around her head served to hide her sorrow from others at the funeral. Now she removed it and folded it into her purse, but her large sunglasses still hid her eyes from her father.

Mike suddenly spoke. "Your grandmother was a kind human being, Julia." His voice was filled with sadness. "Van was always thinking of others; she always thought of herself last after taking care of everyone else. As you could see, even with her death she also helped us, as her death has brought us back together."

Julia was silent, tears falling down her cheeks behind the tinted lenses. Still standing across the livingroom, Mike continued to express the same sentiments, "Julia, our family was a happy one. The four of us were in a circle of love. Two have left us already. Life is full of surprises—both smooth sailing and rough roads. My fear is that if we cannot fix this falling-out, someday you and I will not have the opportunity to talk to each other again."

Julia felt her breath tighten in her throat. Why did she have trouble breathing? Was it that Van was visiting upon her, making her pay attention to her father's words?

Mike spoke again. "You know the charitable foundation that

grandmother and your mother created in Vietnam, to build an orphanage and school? Now that Van has passed, this foundation needs a new leader. Van was hoping you would be that person."

"I know, father." Julia responded. "Grandmother and I talked about it. I said I would accept responsibility at the right time. Yes, I will assume that role."

"That would be wonderful, Julia. Van was the type of person that worked without fanfare. She never bragged about the good things she accomplished. As you know, she returned to Vietnam several times, and besides our support she inspired other families to support it. The foundation has saved many lives. Her hard work and generosity has given wonderful new life opportunities to over a thousand children. She was a living representative of the Buddha."

"I miss grandmother," Julia said plaintively, in a child-like voice.

Mike nodded. "She was a strong lady, like your mother."

"And Jennifer—she is also like that, correct?"

Mike looked into Julia's eyes from across the room. Maintaining an even tone of voice he said, "Yes, Julia. Jennifer *is* a giving and generous lady. That is her nature. I am sorry that you can't see her true character. Whatever irrational emotions, loss of trust, or identity crisis you are going through, these have clearly clouded your judgment."

Julia did not say anything. Obviously he was right.

Julia's mind was in turmoil. She knew her severe behavior had impacted her father and grandmother, causing them both great pain. She might even have contributed to Van's heart condition. Her fear of losing Mike, and in particular her secret taboo love that no daughter should feel, had turned her into a terrible person.

Mike spoke again, "Your grandmother was so looking forward to your graduation play. *Hamlet* was Shakespeare's most famous play. You will make a brilliant Ophelia. I am very sorry she has to miss it, but I am going to be right there, in a front-row seat, cheering you on."

"Thank you, father. It's just two weeks away. I hope grandmother will be looking down from heaven. I need her strength. Her inspiration means the world to me."

After hearing Julia speak, Mike's emotional pain deepened. He realized that Julia's future was at stake, that she was headed in a bad direction, and that it was his responsibility to prevent her from going down the wrong path.

Mike agonized. What could he do? His tiny daughter of past years had grown into a rebellious young lady. A shiver flashed through his body as he remembered young Julia as being a very happy girl once—until the devastating car accident that took the life of her beloved mother Phuong Ha, right in front of her. Following the accident, the lingering shock had intensely impacted Julia psychologically, and from that day Julia had largely become silent and somber. For years he had tried to make her happy again. Knowing that she was afraid of being abandoned he had promised to never leave her. All their lives they had been close, and always confided in each other. However, since Jennifer came into his life Julia had become like a shadow, no longer confiding in him, and even avoiding him.

Apart from himself, for Julia there had only been Van in whom she could share her deep thoughts. Now Van has departed; half their small family of four gone forever! Mike did not want any tragic incidents to happen to them again. He knew that Julia needed his help, but he did not know how to keep her from running away from him again. He felt helpless and guilty when it came to Julia. How he wished that Van was still here, right now, to give him some of her good advice.

Finally, with tears streaming down, in a deeply emotional voice, Mike said, "Julia. My princess. Van reminded me that I was the one who raised you to become what you are today. I have always been so very proud of you. The way you have been acting lately is not what I would have expected from you, but whatever I did to make you act that way, let's fix it together. Please realize, Julia, that whatever I taught you was what I believed would bring out the best in you, and be the best *for* you."

Julia stood there, frozen, paralyzed by her father's words. Those words were like repeated incisions into the wound that she had been trying to heal. Julia had always felt, from the bottom of her heart, that Mike was not only her father but also her most important *friend*. As a father she thought she had owned him, but knew he was not hers to possess. As a friend, she thought she *could* possess him, but she had been so very wrong. At this moment all she wanted was to not suffer any more pain or loss.

Trying to control her emotions, despite her inner confusion and regret, Julia gave Mike a forced and painful smile. Looking straight at him, she spoke carefully and with as much control as she could muster. "Papa, you are the best father I could have ever wished for—that any girl could ever wish for! Please know this!" Then, without looking back, Julia ran out the front door and ducked into a waiting car.

Vans death had caused Julia to panic, and then, to begin to awaken. While she still had many unresolved feelings to process, she accepted the realization that responsibility for the orphanage was now in her hands. She was determined to at least fulfill that responsibility as a mature woman.

"I love you father," she whispered to herself, as her car sped away into the night.

Chapter Thirty

The Play's the Thing...

Igor stood center stage. His eyes gazed at the faces of his students, who stared back at him. A sense of urgency filled his face. They all looked tense. Earlier in that month he had held auditions to determine the leads and supporting roles for the graduation production of *Hamlet*. The try-outs had proven competitive. The class had lived up to his expectations. He had taken the time to summarize the plot so that the class understood the roles he has assigning.

He explained, "*Hamlet* is a play in five acts. Hamlet is the Prince of Denmark. He returns home from a trip to find that following the death of his father, King Hamlet his mother, Gertrude, has hastily remarried. Her new husband is Claudius, the brother to the late King; his uncle! What's more, Claudius has seized the throne. Unsettled, Hamlet smells that something is rotten" —the class laughs and someone calls out, "in the State of Denmark". Igor nodded and smiled.

He continued, "On the ramparts of Elsinore Castle, Hamlet encounters a ghost, who hints that Claudius murdered his father, and directs Hamlet to take revenge." He recounted the rest of the story. The main characters include Ophelia, who is in love with Hamlet, but when he rejects her, she goes mad, climbs into a tree, then jumps into the river and drowns.

As Mike forecast, Igor had selected Julia to play that pivotal role—except that, to make a play more interesting and up-to-date, he took out the suicide scene and had Ophelia return at the end for the death scene, one that involved a sword fight which spells the end of King Claudius, of Hamlet, and of Ophelia's brother Laertes, who has reported Claudius' evil deeds to Hamlet in specific detail. Laertes had also come to extract justice on Hamlet for his cruel rejection of Ophelia.

Igor gave the part of Gertrude, Queen of Denmark, to Tammy. And, since Hamlet has few roles for women, he assigned some of the male roles to the women in the class. "Hamlet let men play the roles of women, and in today's world, fair is fair. We can reverse that." The class applauded. He eyed Vicky and Linda. "You fine women will play Rosencrantz and Guildenstern," he said. "Of course you will experience betrayal and execution." He paused. "Sooner or later, everyone gets their just desserts."

The rest of the class laughed, and even Vicky and Linda joined in, not sure what they were laughing at. Igor grinned broadly. "Okay then, most of you have small but pivotal roles. Trust me, when the agents and producers in the audience hear you speak your lines, they're going to hang on every *syllable*. In life, less can be more. This is a major opportunity."

Vicky and Linda were thrilled. At least they had made the cast, and they took Igor's point that the spotlight would center upon them at crucial moments in the play. Each resolved to capitalize on the opportunity. The important thing, they knew, was to be *part of it*.

Igor finally addressed Jason, his Hamlet. Igor's selection honored Jason. "Hamlet is arguably the most famous character in Shakespeare's repertoire. Our greatest actors in history have played him, and brought to this demanding role remarkably original interpretations."

"Thank you, Igor," Jason said, clearly appreciative of the honor he was receiving.

Igor gave him a stern look. "I don't want to see a hip rendition of the prince. Let yourself go. We want to see Hamlet's passion and raw energy as he wrestles with the impossible decisions he must make. We want to *feel* the deaths that he causes, not merely observe them. We have to feel the horror that he brings down upon himself."

Igor took a moment to let the class settle down. "Let me discuss Ophelia," he said. "You all know who I've chosen to play her. There are so many talented students among you," he said diplomatically. "But I think we can all agree that the person who had thrown her heart and soul into the class, who never gave in and never gave up in her efforts to improve, is our very own Julia."

He looked at Julia and applauded her. The rest of the class rose and applauded. The faces of the class betrayed no evidence of cynical rejection. There was sheer admiration. *She was one of them.* Julia was stunned, realizing that her struggles had paid off. Her own largely imaginary stones and arrows had raised towering obstacles to her path in the theatre, and now—finally—she could see a path opening before her eyes.

"I hope I can do the role justice," she almost whispered.

"You can, and you will," Igor told her.

"My English is still not perfect."

"It's damn good. What counts is authenticity. You, my dear Julia, are one-of-a-kind. Ask any agent, any director, any producer. You have what it takes. There's a quality that emanates from deep within you. You're going to be a star."

*****

Backstage, alone in the dressing room and seated at her dressing table, fully decked out in her flowing Ophelia costume, Julia sat, looking at herself in the mirror. She worked on her long hair, weaving two braids on each side, along with some fragrant flowers. Finally satisfied, she refreshed her makeup and began practicing her final lines—the new lines Igor had given her to modernize the play and Ophelia's role.

But tonight something felt wrong. She felt closer to the characters of Hamlet and his uncle Claudius than she did to poor innocent Ophelia. Suddenly a perfectly reasonable thought popped into her head: "I should have played Claudius." After all, she told herself, Claudius, the king's brother, killed his brother out of jealousy, so he could take the throne and have Queen Gertrude for himself. Likewise she, Julia, out of her own jealousy, was eager to destroy Jennifer so she could have her father all to herself. Why, she'd even dreamt of stabbing Jennifer repeatedly until her mortal enemy was dead!

After thinking of how she was like Claudius, she mentally went over her similarities to Hamlet, especially the fact that they both heard voices mocking them: Hamlet from a ghost, Julia from evil spirits—perhaps from the devil himself. She was the embodiment of both these tortured souls, and certainly not the clueless Ophelia!

Julia's feverish thoughts were interrupted by a loud knock, as someone jiggled the knob of the locked dressing room door. Julia shrank back, frightened. What if someone was trying to get in who could discover her secret? Then, to her relief, Bethany's voice wafted into the room: "Ten minutes warning to get onstage, Julia. Are you in there?"

"Yes, it's me, Julia! I will be right out," Julia managed to shout back, still disoriented.

After hearing Bethany's footsteps walk away, Julia rechecked herself in the mirror. Then she stood up on shaky legs, unlocked the door, and stepped into the wings to watch the action from behind a velvet curtain.

On stage Ophelia's brother Laertes was telling Hamlet how Claudius had murdered the king by putting poison in his ear, and that Claudius now planned to poison Hamlet. Hidden behind the curtain, Julia was trying hard to stay focused on her final last scene as Ophelia. In that scene, Ophelia—already driven mad by Hamlet's harsh and undeserved rejection of her—would suffer even more as she witnessed the death of her brother Laertes. As her tension mounted, Julia attempted to distract herself by looking down at the audience. What she saw shocked her. Every face wore an angry or disgusted expression, a reflection of their feelings towards the terrible Claudius. Then Julia heard voices behind her: a group of stagehands were talking about Claudius. "Can you imagine killing your brother to get to his wife? I mean, your own sister-in-law," one said. "Yes, talk about *family ties*. Disgusting," another smirked.

At that moment, already in a fragile state, something snapped in Julia. She had an immediate flashback to the Dr. Drew Show, where the topic had been Genetic Sexual Attraction. She remembered someone saying, "Those sick people. Doesn't anybody have any sense of decency anymore?"

On stage the actors cursed Claudius for his murderous actions. Behind the curtains, they cursed those physically attracted to a family member. Julia's head was spinning. She felt like she was about to faint. "I killed Jennifer's child," she reminded herself. "I made my grandmother so sad that she had a heart attack. I dreamt of killing Jennifer. I must be sick. Everyone must hate me, I *deserve* to be hated."

Putting her hands to her head, Julia tried to press the damning thoughts away, but all she could think of was that she must be cursed. Overwhelming guilt made her feel like she was suffocating. There was not enough oxygen in the air.

Just at that moment, Bethany appeared behind Julia. "Go, Ophelia," her friend said with a cheerful whisper, and gave Julia a gentle push to get her onstage.

In a state of panic, Julia moved from behind the curtain to the very front of the stage, and stood there, frozen. The audience waited expectantly, but Julia was immobile as the curses she had heard, in front and behind her, kept echoing in her head: *"Evil, evil, evil!"*

Then, without warning, Julia yelled out: *"No!" I am not like Claudius. People cannot blame me for being evil. I'm not cursed."* Still at the front of the stage, her eyes searched for Mike until she found him.

What was wrong with Julia? From his seat in the front row Mike, stared up at his daughter, deeply confused. Then their eyes locked. For Julia, deep in her vortex of grief and regret, the fact that Jennifer was seated beside her father did not register. She focused only on her father's eyes. Without conscious thought her soliloquy began to tumble out of her.

"Father, please forgive me for everything. For being a selfish, thoughtless girl. For wanting more love from you, and a different kind of love, than I should ever have wanted. For being obsessed with you."

What was this? Ophelia talking to her father? Was this some sort of modern take on *Hamlet*? The audience began to mumble. "What is she saying?" people asked each other. The actors on stage were frozen in place. Julia saw and heard nothing. She just continued:

"Because father, perhaps you have guessed by now: I not only loved you: I was in love with you. I wanted to be my mother. I wanted to be your wife. I made you and grandma and Jennifer very unhappy because of it. I am so sorry for what I put you through. You did not deserve it. There are no excuses. All I can say is, it was a kind of

sickness, and now I am going away to heal. Please be happy with your Jennifer. I want your happiness. You gave me a great life, and I will always treasure those wonderful years we had together, as father and daughter. And soon I must leave, and fulfill my destiny."

Paralyzed in his seat, Mike took in her words, and finally understood the secret his beloved daughter had been struggling with for so long. A tidal wave of sadness washed over him. *That poor child. That poor young woman. What had he done wrong to make this happen? How could they fix this*, he asked himself.

On stage Jason—understanding that something was seriously jeopardizing the performance—jumped in to help Julia, and at the same time do what he could to save the play. Unsheathing his sword, he went over to the actor playing Claudius, threw him to the ground, and ran his pretend sword through him. Next he turned to Laertes and initiated a sword fight. Laertes fought back with his own sword. Soon both of them were mortally wounded and the audience was re-engaged in the play.

Now fully aware of where she was, Julia, mercifully forgetting for the moment everything she had just said and done, became Ophelia again, and rushed over to cradle her brother in her arms as he died. With that, the play ended, and the curtain came down—only to rise again shortly for curtain calls.

In the front row, Mike sat without moving, not bothering to brush away his tears. Immeasurably sad for his deeply troubled daughter, he silently whispered, " I love you, Princess." He would find her backstage and assure her that everything was going to be okay, that he understood why she had acted as she did. Most of all, he would assure her that he loved her no less than before, and that he would get her any help she needed.

On stage, after Jason had taken his final much-deserved bows, the audience eagerly waited for Julia to emerge to receive *her* accolades. Moments passed. No one knew where "Ophelia" was. The actress who played her, Julia Chamonix, had disappeared.

Chapter Thirty One

After fleeing from the theatre Julia had rushed home, found her passport and other necessary papers, and hastily filled two large suitcases, a makeup case and a carry-on bag on wheels with as much of her belongings as they would hold. She had no intention of ever returning. There was nothing left for her here, at what felt like the lowest point in her life. She called a car service to take her to JFK Airport, planning to take the first plane she could get. If there were no flights today she would stay at an airport hotel overnight. She had made her confession and she was not sorry. But after that, how could she ever face her father again?

Over time, her journey back to Vietnam became successful on many levels, but it had not been easy. Slowly she built sturdy pillars for a new life. Starting in Ho Chi Minh City, she did as her grandmother had wished, and took the helm of the foundation. All of Vietnam was growing fast, poverty was widespread, and there were so many children in need. Julia's energy and enthusiasm strengthened the organization and broadened it's support. However, the large numbers of children she served through her family foundation had many complicated needs. Often there was not enough time or money to do all that was needed to keep them healthy, well fed, well clothed, educated and thriving. Nonetheless, Julia persevered, and made what many considered remarkable progress.

Her time in Vietnam also enabled her to pursue the important dream—to become a singer, even composing her own songs and music. Julia had picked up the ability to play a piano through an intuitive sensibility for treble and base clefs. She could imitate any tune by ear. Soon enough she realized that she had a lovely soprano voice. She began by singing her mother's favorite lullabies to the orphans.

After performing at one fundraiser, a top Vietnamese music producer approached and asked if she was Phuong Ha's daughter, because her face looked exactly like Phuong Ha's. The mother-daughter resemblance was remarkable! Her affirmative response—and clear singing talent—led to a recording session. The producer loved her work. Working with her closely, they produced a successful first album.

The album and the music video that accompanied its release—struck Vietnam like a lightning bolt. Julia's family legacy provided the platform for a strong promotional campaign. Within six months she had emerged as a star in her own right. Her most popular recordings included her own new compositions. Julia's newest compositions reached a younger audience, and generated significant income to help support and even expand the work of the foundation. Later, new albums included songs her mother had recorded.

A UNICEF report singled Julia out for her work with children. As one news report pointed out, "Thanks to this unique star, thousands of children who might have been left to the ill fortunes of grinding poverty, including homelessness and abuse, have instead been brought up in a loving, safe environment, received good educations and realistic opportunities for wonderful, productive futures."

On a personal level, Jason had tracked Julia down. He worked hard to stay in close touch with her. Their acting school production of *Hamlet* had, thanks to Igor, been seen by the casting agents and directors he had invited to attend, after telling them they were going to see a future star. Clearly they agreed. After his triumphant performance Jason received an invitation to try out for an action thriller from Paramount Studios opposite Ryan Gosling—and got the part! He told Julia all his news, and she enthusiastically responded. Despite the distance, the two former classmates began to email, text, and Skype frequently. After a while they would get on the phone regularly, and talk for hours.

About a year and a half after Julia first arrived in Vietnam Jason surprised her with a visit. Her surprise turned to astonishment and delight when he announced that his film had wrapped, and, rather than accept any more offers at this time, he was prepared to stay and help her with her work.

They married in a ceremony at the orphanage. Their wedding had been a joyful occasion, but small and quiet. They had not even told their respective families about the wedding, opting instead to eventually hold a second ceremony in New York.

That was how, two and half years after Julia had fled the theatre, and one year after Jason joined her in Vietnam, the happy couple found themselves on the way back to their "other home" in the U.S.

As the Singapore Airlines 747 jumbo jet descended through billowy clouds, and the outlines of Manhattan came into view, Julia clasped Jason's hand and put her other hand on her stomach. The baby they were expecting had began to move inside her. Everything about her pregnancy—and this trip—filled her with anticipation and a sense of possibility. She reflected back on the past years and how, with time, deep reflection, and committing herself to helping children in need, she had regained her sense of self and gotten over her then inappropriate feelings that had caused so much heartache for everyone. Of course her happiness with Jason had also contributed to her newfound peace of mind and maturity.

Sitting next to Jason in the luxurious business class section of the jumbo jet, she looked at her new husband with great affection, but also concern.

"Jason, I know they'll be waiting for us, but do you think they'll really be happy to see us? I told you all the hateful things I did. I don't know if they can ever truly forgive me."

"Julia, stop. That's all water under the bridge. They'll be delighted," he assured her. "And the icing on the cake is—you and I have some big career opportunities in New York."

Julia's well-connected Vietnamese producer had lined up a New York agent for her. The agent's team had already mapped out a plan to introduce her music to the Big Apple and then to the rest of North America. The initial response to her beautiful voice, stunning appearance and acting talent, which showed itself in her music videos on YouTube and throughout the internet, had been wildly positive. In the meantime, Jason was preparing to play *Hamlet* on Broadway. He would also sign a contract the following week for an action thriller that would pair him with Bruce Willis and Jennifer Lawrence.

Emerging from customs, Julia and Jason spotted Mike and Jennifer, eagerly waiting outside the baggage claims area. With them, sitting comfortably upright in a lovely red stroller, was their daughter, Jessica, barely 11 months old. Open arms awaited Jason and Julia as the family reunited.

"You look wonderful, Julia," Mike said, hugging his daughter. Then he put his hand on her swollen mid-section. At six months along, Julia's pregnancy was obvious. "I see our family numbers are growing," he beamed.

"And I see that they already have," Julia said, grinning radiantly as she bent down to greet the little tow-headed toddler. "Hello Jessica. I'm your big sister Julia. And you will soon have a little nephew named Jim to play with and love." The child smiled back, reached out her hand, and touched Julia's nose.

They all laughed, and Jennifer and Julia embraced. As they exited the busy airport, Julia had a sudden realization. The feeling of not belonging fully in one culture or the other had vanished, like a bad dream. She would always be Eurasian: half Vietnamese and half American. What mattered most was that she was now one hundred percent *Julia*.

The little girl who had suffered from the tragic loss of her mother and had clung to her father no longer felt the need to prove anything to anyone. "I am enough," she told herself, gazing upon the beaming faces of her husband, her father, her father's loving wife, and their child—her sister. *No halves here*, she smiled to herself. Patting her stomach, right at the spot where the little boy was growing inside her, she walked up to the double doors that led to the street. Jason and Mike each opened a door for her, but Julia stepped aside, gesturing to Jennifer to push the stroller through first.

"After you," she said.

The wonderful thing, she thought, as she walked out of the airport with her family, was that who she, Julia, was—had been there all the time.

Sometimes it takes a breakdown to create a breakthrough.

·